Piping Down

the Valleys Wild

MAXINE HART

Northwoods Press

ISBN 0-89002-145-7, Paperback
ISBN 0-89002-146-5, Cloth

Library of Congress Catalog Card Number: 80-81363

Also by Maxine Hart:

A NEST OF DRAGONS

NORTHWOODS PRESS
PO Box 249
Stafford, VA 22554 USA

For Bob

Piping Down the Valleys Wild

1

I first saw Sandy one afternoon early this summer as I was driving by a wooded area and my eye was caught by a glimpse of a tall, naked figure dancing in the woods and playing a pipe, like a faun, like the Greek god, Pan. Intrigued, I backed the car and looked again and decided to go into the woods to see him up close, to find out who he was and what he was doing there.

I hoped the old Dodge would not break its springs on the bumpy trails in there. It belonged to Fritz and I hated him, but I simply have to drive sometimes or I'll go out of my mind. I knew that I shouldn't be driving into the woods, though, and I knew that I should have learned a lesson about strangers after my last experience with one. And I knew that Aunt Sue would not approve if she knew. I drove in and there, in a clearing, was my woodland creature, but he wasn't dancing.

He was waving a long piece of string in the air, and this confused me until I saw that he seemed to be measuring the distance between two trees. I wondered why I had thought that he was dancing and playing a flute and asked myself if I wanted to know a pagan god. He hadn't even turned around to look at me and I knew that he had heard the car. It would have been impossible not to unless he was deaf. His ears—I wished they were a little bit pointed. Perhaps if I could see them at close range....

His bare back was slender and browned—his white shirt was tossed on the blanket spread out on the ground beside him—and his trousers were tan. (I hadn't *really* thought he was naked, of course.) His head was well shaped. Then he turned to face me and I saw that he was remarkably handsome. His eyes were almost as black as his hair and his expression, while not welcoming, was pleasant. I looked away, at a loss, feeling suddenly awkward and intrusive. His car, parked several feet away, was a sporty white dream. Usually I notice cars and his, so unusual and fine, had been there all along, but I had been so taken up with staring at him that the car had not registered.

I couldn't just sit there. I slid out from behind the wheel and walked toward him. What could I say, what approach would interest him, would make me feel less of a fool? Closer, his good looks unnerved me and I found myself talking too rapidly, heard my own voice beating in my ears as I told him the truth, that I had come on an impulse, out of curiosity, that he had seemed like a faun dancing in the woods. I stopped abruptly and my face grew warm. He was nineteen, I thought, or twenty, an ideal type, and he must think me demented.

His expression did not change except for a slight frown. He seemed to be thinking over what I had said. Finally, he asked mildly, "F-a-w-n or f-a-u-n?"

"Like Pan," I told him, noticing then that his ears were not at all pointed but that his eyes had a very slight slant. "With a reed pipe."

He nodded. We stood there and looked at each other. He seemed at ease but I was uncomfortable, wanting so much to stay there with him, drawn to him, and knowing that I should leave, feeling certain that I would be sent away, dismissed by indifference. I had a strange, quick feeling that this young man was not one to involve himself.

In another moment I would have to climb into the old Dodge and back up and turn and go, and the thought of this made my chest hurt. I had somehow got all emotional about him, and I wanted to stay so much that I could have wept. And yet, what could I do? I am a certain way—that is, I have to feel that I am wanted—and without encouragement I would have to be on my way. I stood waiting for the pain to subside so that I could move. I wanted to be able to say goodbye and not merely wheel and go without a word, like a boor.

His dark, intelligent eyes held mine. It was a delicate moment, and I had no real hope. Then he said, "How far would you guess it is between those two trees?" He indicated the ones he had measured with his string. "How many feet?"

My heart started to pump again, sluggishly, as if my blood had thickened. The delicate moment was past and I had been saved. A crisis was over, I could stay here now, and I honestly felt that I had been reborn. I'd never felt like this before in my life, and I wasn't sure that I could handle this new feeling.

I was taking so long to answer that I was afraid he would think me stupid, but with the pain gone, I felt slow and heavy. Luckily, his own speech was slow and measured, and he spoke again. "Would it be right for a hammock?"

"Oh, yes," I said, desperately wanting to please him and not even looking at the trees. Whatever the space was, I would fix up the hammock to fit it. I am fairly good with my hands and I would work hard to make everything fit properly. I knew it would be all right. It would have to be. "Yes," I repeated, not so brightly this time but with more authority, and he dropped the string and smiled.

If I had needed a push in his direction, which I did not, the smile would have done nicely. It was a smile of such sweetness, and I felt the impact of it so that I didn't trust myself to say a word, and I couldn't find the power to move a muscle in my face to begin an answering smile. I simply stood there numbly until he spoke again.

"Will you have lunch with me?" He gestured toward the blanket where, beside his shirt, was a large, brown-leather picnic hamper.

"Thank you." I remember that I sounded shy, but I followed him quickly enough to the blanket. He had asked me to eat with him, to share his food, and so he must be attracted to rather than repelled by me. He must like me at least a little. I was grateful.

The contents of the hamper startled me, at first with the quantity and then with the quality. "There's always too much," he said, seeing my reaction. He put on his shirt, buttoning even the top button but forgetting to tuck in the tails, and added, "I leave most of the food for the squirrels."

"It's delicious." Tiny Cornish hens stuffed with wild rice, a rare treat at our house, a colorful fruit salad with a creamy, whipped dressing I'd never tasted before, buttery croissants, and pastel-iced, chocolate petits fours. All this he took for granted in a picnic lunch intended to be solitary, and then left most of it for squirrels! I looked again at his car gleaming where the sun touched it. Not only was this boy beautiful and kind, but he was also rich. He was too good to be true, and I was suddenly sad enough to have to blink back tears. My eyelids felt hot and raw. He was beyond me, I could never hope to interest someone like him, not seriously, and yet no one else would seem good enough now. It was depressing, and I was afraid that I wouldn't be able to swallow the piece of little game hen which had started on its way down my throat.

"Forgive me. I'm slow." He poured from a leather flask that looked like an ancient goatskin and handed me a cup of what I thought must be wine.

"Bacchus," I said, without really meaning to say it aloud, and drank, washing down the hen. It was grape juice, but light and sparkly, like red champagne.

"F-a-u-n." He smiled again and added, "It's Sandy, actually."

At first I didn't understand that he was introducing himself, as the name did not tie in with his dark hair and eyes and skin. Sandy should mean reddish-blond hair, gray-blue eyes, and probably freckles. But he did not seem to mind my hesitation, and his smile faded so gradually that I knew he was not impatient or annoyed, only waiting with interest for however I would respond.

Finally, I said, "Is your name Alexander, then?"

"How did you know?" He seemed genuinely surprised and after another long, thoughtful look asked, "Do you know me?"

"No. I just thought that Sandy was a nickname for Alexander."

"Oh." It was his turn again to think and as usual he took his time about it. In someone who was not as good looking as Sandy, this slowness would probably have been quite annoying, at least until I got used to it. "No. It's a nickname for Sanford, my middle name." There was another pause, but I waited patiently now, too. I was adjusting to his unhurried manner. "My name is Alexander Sanford Carlyle III."

He said this the way most boys I knew would say, "Hi, I'm Bill Smith." Sandy was simply giving me information and I knew, too, that Aunt Sue would say that "the third" meant only that he had a father and a grandfather with the same name, but I was still impressed, although I tried not to show it. I knew that showing it would puzzle him and possibly make him think less of me. I offered my hand and said, "Hello, Sandy, I'm Gloria Thatcher Elliott, and everyone calls me Gay."

He took my hand briefly and without speaking or smiling, but it seemed to me that he was pleased. I thought that I had so far been lucky enough to have made a decent impression on him in spite of barging in on his sanctuary, but I was completely unprepared for his next statement.

"I'd like you to meet my mother," he said, as matter-of-factly as he had said that there was always too much food in his hamper. "She'd like you, I know."

"Why—why, thank you." I was terribly confused, at first wondering if he was making fun of me and immediately seeing that he was not. "I—that is—it's a nice compliment."

"We wouldn't have to go to her today," he said and poured some more grape juice into my cup. "Where do you live, Gay?"

I told him about Aunt Sue's rooming house on the east side of the city, about my parents' and then my brother's deaths when I was twelve, and that I had spent the last five years with Aunt Sue.

"Twelve and five. You're seventeen, Gay?"

"I will be, in August." I answered all of his slow, deliberate questions, telling him that I had just graduated from high school and that I planned to go to the state university in September but that I wasn't certain why. I mean, I had no special interest and no reason for planning on more school except that I'd always liked to read and got good grades. It was really that I had nothing else in particular to do with the next few years of my life and college seemed better than a job filing and clerking and typing somewhere. I would have to have jobs like that to help pay tuition and expenses—Aunt Sue had little enough—but at least, after an education, I could look forward to more interesting and better-paid labor.

I was about to add something I'd never have admitted to Velma or my other friends—that I was looking forward to learning new things, discovering new books and ideas, knowing people who had less limited ways of viewing the world—when Sandy said, "You could get married."

If Harold had said that, I'd've known that he meant married to *him*, and I'd've been annoyed, but Sandy's saying it threw me off balance, mainly, I think, because in the back of my mind, always, when I saw a boy, there was the thought of him as a possible husband for me. This thought was never serious or pressing, but it was there and tended to embarrass me a little, making me wonder why I could not manage to feel more secure in life. I could surely take care of myself and not depend upon a man. I felt that I was supposed to enjoy life and not worry about catching a mate.

Anyway, I knew that I did not want to marry Harold but I was not at all sure that I didn't want to marry Sandy. I was terribly attracted to him and I didn't want to frighten him by showing it.

"Well, but who—I mean, I'm not really old enough to marry anyone," I said when I realized that he was waiting for an answer. He never seemed to say anything without thought and he was a wonderful listener, giving me his entire attention, but I realized, too, that I wasn't learning anything about *his* background and I wanted to know everything about him, everything from the moment he was born until now. "How about you?" I asked, steering away from the subject of marriage. "How do you feel about college?"

He shrugged and smiled. "I've been there." He seemed to withdraw then, as if he had lost interest in the conversation. I began another question but he cut in with, "How would you like to go for a ride?"

"In *that* car? Oh, good heavens, yes!"

On the ride I discovered a flaw in him. He was not a particularly good driver. That is, his judgment seemed off, as if he wasn't quite sure where the right side of the road began or, as Aunt Sue would put it, he took his half in the middle. The traffic was very light, though, and I didn't really worry. I mean, I know I would have jumped at the chance anyway when we came to a turn-off about ten miles down the highway and he stopped and asked if I'd like to drive back.

His car, a Jaguar convertible, was a joy to handle. I couldn't stop smiling, it was such a pleasure to drive it, to be sitting next to Sandy in a machine like that, to have such a lovely beginning with him.

Back in the woods again, he said, "You do that well."

I think I blushed a little. The day was so sweet and exciting.

"You can drive all the time, if you like," he told me, his eyes lighter now, almost nutmeg-colored in the sun. "Your touch is better than mine."

By that time I had adjusted to him well enough so that I did not protest. In his directness, in what I thought of as his sophisticated simplicity, an insincere remark from me would only confuse him and perhaps make him wary of me. So I said, "All right, I'd like to, Sandy," and he smiled.

While we had been gone the pampered squirrels had attacked the remains of our feast, including one whole stuffed hen which we had not even touched. "What a waste!"

He glanced at me, then shrugged and shook out the blanket. "We'll have more tomorrow." He tossed the empty hamper into the back seat and I heard a kind of strangled little sound. Curiously, I turned and, seeing the guitar on the floor, lifted it. One string was still vibrating.

"Yours, Sandy? Do you play it?" When he nodded, I held it out to him. "Will you play something for me?"

"Of course."

I don't know the name of the song—I asked and he told me and even discussed its history, but I've forgotten it all except that it originated in India—but it was like nothing I'd ever heard, different and haunting. I play only a little, but even I could tell that he was a master of the instrument. It would do anything for him.

I stood by the car for a while, dazzled and dreaming and watching while Sandy, like a silent study in slow motion, folded the blanket, seeming to concentrate on each movement involved in the task.

When I said that I should be going along home, he didn't urge me to stay but asked, "Shall we come here tomorrow?"

"Yes." I didn't hesitate or make any conditions. My God, the relief of not having to pretend to have to break another date, the relief of not having to play the trite, coy game which, I admit, I had not until then found quite so disgusting.

"I'll come to your house in the morning." He gave me a notebook and pencil and waited while I wrote directions. "At ten?"

"Good." I got back into the Dodge, dismissed, I knew, but how royally!

2

I eased into the parking space in front of the house, the one Fritz prefers, as in small things like that I try to please him. I baby sat quite a lot and always had spending money for gas, but it would've taken a century to save enough for a car, so I depended on Fritz's generosity with the Dodge.

Not that he was really generous, of course, and we both knew it. His car was the only thing he had that I wanted any part of and he kept trying to give me more, like movie tickets and pats on my backside. He was about forty and unattractive and terribly persistent. He was a foreman in a pickle factory on Farnes Street and he kept offering me a job there as one of his "girls." I would have to be starving, and even then — !

I was a little late bringing the car back and I knew he'd be miffed. I knocked on his door and waited, knowing that he'd keep me standing there for a while, as he had to make himself feel important in little ways. He was the only man in the house at the time and the only roomer on the first floor, but his room was separated from Aunt Sue's part by the entry hall and staircase so that we didn't have to see him very often. (It's the room Rennie and I shared when we first came here, before he died and I moved in closer to Aunt Sue.)

The downstairs of the house is kind of cut up. Aunt Sue and I have a living room, kitchen, a bathroom and our bedrooms. Mine used to be the pantry and Aunt Sue's used to be the dining room, and even though our quarters are far from elaborate, they are cozy and clean.

There are five bedrooms and two baths upstairs, and whenever the lady guests complain about the hot water running out before everyone has had a chance at it, Aunt Sue counters by mentioning the plumbing bills she has to pay because of all the long hair that gets tangled in the drains. ''More hot water would mean more shampoos and that would mean more shedded hair and more stopped-up drains and more bills, and more bills would mean raising the rent.''

For some reason this always makes Miss Mayhew nod her head and murmur, ''A rose is a rose is a rose.'' Then she and Aunt Sue smile at each other, but it seems to me that the joke or whatever it is goes on and on, too.

Fortunately, there is a small half bath at the end of Fritz's hall and he used that and stayed on the first floor. With his habit of pinching backsides, the ladies upstairs would have gone stark raving out of their minds.

He finally opened the door and I gave him the car keys and said heartily, ''Thanks a lot, Fritz. I filled the tank.''

''That a fact?'' Usually he stood around with his mouth a little open and spit collecting at the corners. As Aunt Sue put it, he was probably smart enough, but from the look of him he couldn't pound sand down a rat hole. But right then he was scowling like mad. ''That why you're so late? You knew I wanted the car at three sharp.''

I hate to be jumped on when I know I deserve it even more than when I don't have it coming, so I snatched a kleenex out of my purse and sniffed into it. Corny sarcasm was the only effective way to snap back at him, as he never knew how to handle it. ''Thanks again,'' I told him then, and started to walk down the hall.

''Hold on, kid.'' He pulled me back and a big friendly grin almost split his face in two. ''What're you always in such a hurry about?''

He leaned toward me and I could see that the old fool had finally got up the nerve to try to kiss me. The thought was pretty sickening and I jerked my arm away.

''All right for you,'' he called after me, like a six-year-old. ''Just wait till you want the car again, babe.''

I kept on walking without answering or turning around, but I was worried. Without wheels, I was going to feel all tensed up.

As I passed the stairs I heard someone cough. ''Oh, hello there, Miss Mayhew.'' She had asked me to call her by her first name, but I couldn't remember it—something a little complicated, like Deirdre or Adrienne.

She stood blinking at the top of the stairs, reminding me of somebody who's just come out of a dark movie into the sun, still in the mood of the story and not yet adjusted to the outside world. ''It's you, Gay,'' she said. ''I didn't reckonize you at first.''

Miss Mayhew was proud of her vocabulary and tried to be precise in her speech, but she always left the g out of recognize. And the reason she didn't ''reckonize'' people was that she was near-sighted and refused to wear her glasses. Or maybe she just kept forgetting them, for all I know.

''It's a beautiful day,'' I said so that I wouldn't seem too abrupt—I was dying to get to my room and be alone and think of Sandy—and went on down the hall.

Aunt Sue was in the kitchen, shelling peas. I don't know anyone else who shells peas, but she says that fresh peas are not only less expensive than frozen ones but better tasting and more fun.

What she means by fun is interesting and a little strange. She doesn't *believe* that inanimate objects have a soul or feelings, but once in a while when she tips over a bottle, for example, she'll set it straight and then give it a little pat, almost as though she's letting it know she's sorry. Or she'll be shelling peas and put the pods in rows and choose each one in order, just as if they'd been waiting in line for their turn. I mean, she wouldn't consider taking a pod ahead of one that had been "waiting" since the waiting pod might have its feelings hurt. She often treats things like people even though she knows better. And she does know. She never gets this game of hers confused with reality.

At first I thought she was eccentric but I learned that it was a part of her love for everything and her need to be kind and fair.

I'll always be grateful to Aunt Sue for giving me love when I needed it. When our parents were killed, Rennie and I would have been completely lost without her. And when Rennie died and I needed love very badly, she was there to give it to me.

Love is the one thing in the world I absolutely cannot do without. I have to have somebody to care about and to care about me and be *involved* with me. I think I would die without that.

Aunt Sue looked up from the peas and asked, "Nice drive?"

"Mm hmm." I never mentioned Fritz's behavior, of course, and I wasn't in the least bit ready to tell her about Sandy. I wanted to keep him all to myself for a while and, anyway, I knew she'd have duckfits about the way I'd met him, so I said, "I think Miss Mayhew's on her way in for coffee."

"No, she was here just a while ago. Drank three cups," she added with satisfaction. Her coffee is always good.

Aunt Sue could charge her lady roomers more if she'd give them kitchen privileges, but she would rather have the privacy and also the order and cleanliness.

But she likes to have her guests, as she calls the

roomers, drop in for cups of coffee and tea and cocoa and she is willing to stop in the middle of almost anything to plug in the percolator or turn on the gas under the teakettle and sit down at the kitchen table with another middle-aged lady and sip and chat. I guess she is never lonely.

"What time is Harold coming?" she asked. "It must be weeks since I've seen him."

"Eight-thirty." I'd almost forgotten about my date with Harold. I hadn't wanted to go out with him, but he'd been so insistent and so enthusiastic about a "surprise" he had for me that I'd agreed. I liked him and he was a wonderful dancer, but he'd become very serious about us this last year, and I was determined to get away from people like him who were nice but nothing special and just as ignorant as I was.

In my room and alone at last, I picked up my guitar. It was tinny and beat-up compared with Sandy's, but so was my playing. I had taught myself a few chords by watching some lessons on an educational TV program, but of course I wasn't good and wouldn't have dreamed of playing when anyone else could hear.

I strummed and sang a song that seemed to come naturally just then:

"Black, black, black is the color of my true love's hair
His lips are wondrous rosy fair
The handsomest face and the gentlest hands
I love the ground whereon he stands."

A lovely, lovely song, but a too romantic choice. Songs like that make me fall in love faster, and I knew that I was going to love Sandy. A devastating song like that would only speed it up and I couldn't afford that. I needed all my wits, all the cool I could hang on to, because I was way out of my depth this time, and I could easily drown.

And yet, I wanted to go ahead and drown.

I reached for my bathrobe. I always stayed a half hour in the tub. Aunt Sue preferred showers, saying the purpose was to get in, get clean, and get out, but I love to soak. And sometimes I can collect my thoughts in all that soap and water and bubblebath.

I was in a real daze about Sandy and sure that I'd never come out of it. He was not only handsome and talented, but he was different from anyone else I'd ever known. What other *male* would voluntarily admit that I drove better than he did and then turn his car over to me? That alone was incredible, but he was different in other ways, too, in his deliberate speech and movements, in his reactions and frankness and sincerity.

That bit about meeting his mother. No boy I'd ever met would say a thing like that unless he was the world's biggest square or had serious intentions, like Harold. Of course it could also be a new approach, a line, but not from Sandy. His saying that had given me a real jolt, and it made me so nervous, thinking about meeting his mother, that I scooped up a handful of bubbles and began to *chew* on them. I actually was tensed up enough to do this until the bitter taste of the suds brought me back to earth.

I told myself then that since I couldn't judge Sandy's words or behavior by the ordinary standards of people I was used to, I must realize that he had probably noticed some small things about me that he thought his mother would like and had simply mentioned it. It had been a casual remark, soon forgotten, but I was glad that he had found something especially good about me.

What could I offer him? I wasn't beautiful, brilliant, or clever, or sparkling, and I had wondered for years whether or not I had real character. I knew that I didn't have a great deal of courage, for example. I was scared to death inside about going to college—could I make it? And would the grind of a job and study be worth it to me?

Would I stick it out? Would I even make a start? It would be so much easier to stay here and work at a routine job for a while and then marry Harold or one of the others and never worry about taking care of myself or learning anything.

But I knew I would worry about what I was missing, and the question was, did I have what it took to go out on my own and get an education?

Also, I knew that I was selfish and squeamish and a quitter. Last summer I read an article in the paper about some blind, retarded children, and I felt I had to do something for them. So I called and made an appointment and went to the Home with boxes of candy. They loved the candy and drooled all over it. I tried to talk to them and got exactly nowhere. They were very badly retarded and seemed to understand almost nothing. Then I tried reading to them out of one of their books, but their faces stayed blank so half way through I gave up. I played records for them and some of them smiled a little, but mostly they just slobbered over the candy. I hate to admit this, but those kids were repulsive. I never went back.

Every week for two months after that I sent two dollars to Miss Compton with a note asking her to buy a box of candy for the children, but this was simply to make myself feel better. What is known as a sop to the conscience, I guess. Then at Christmas I sent ten dollars, and nothing since although it was June again. I spent my money selfishly, on gas and clothes and other things for myself and to tell the truth I was trying to forget those kids. My do-good-unto-others phase didn't last very long. It was like an attack of fever that cooled off.

I knew that most people thought of me as a "nice girl"—that is, responsible and well-behaved, but in this day and age these qualities often add up to winning the booby prize while someone like Velma who is sassy and openly undependable and kind of exciting walks off with the goldplated cup.

And I could understand why. I mean, if I was somebody else I would enjoy her company more than my own, I think, because she can keep a bantering conversation going and she always has ideas on daring, fun things to do.

Sandy, I thought, must be used to girls who were like that but with more quality and without Velma's tactlessness and fairly shallow thinking.

I guess she is better looking than I am, too. Harold said once that this was the craziest opinion I'd had yet, but he was so prejudiced in my favor that I couldn't trust his judgment. Velma's red hair and green eyes and a spatter of freckles across her nose make her vivid, but my hair is plain light brown—it has a natural wave and with a good cut it stays neat without fussing, but on the other hand, it never looks terrific—and my eyes are light blue which is never dramatic like dark blue or dark brown or green.

My skin is clear and my teeth are straight, but I don't have pink cheeks and my smile doesn't *flash*. My figure is okay—good arms and legs and a small waist—but not petite and gamine or statuesque and regal, just medium. My best feature is the shape of my face, which is just round enough, I think, with bones in the right places, and saves me from utter mediocrity.

Altogether, I thought I was above average but not nearly at Sandy's level. I needed a special quality, and the only one, the only single thing I had to offer was my feeling for him. Any rival would have to be giving off sparks to like him more than I did.

Aunt Sue was baking a cake, and the spicy smell of it drifting into the bathroom began to make me hungry. Apparently even love wasn't going to make me lose my appetite. Before today, I would have said that I knew something about food. Aunt Sue was a marvelous cook and had taught me how to buy and prepare and also to appreciate food, but Sandy's lunch had made me realize how limited my knowledge was.

My thoughts circled back to our picnic in the woods. Sandy had said, "You can drive all the time, if you like." Didn't that mean he planned to see me quite a lot? I daydreamed happily for quite a while until I finally noticed that my hands were getting waterlogged and it was time to abandon the tub.

At eight-thirty sharp Harold rang the doorbell. He was always right on time and for once I didn't keep him waiting in the living room while I tore around my room wondering why I never started to get dressed sooner since I knew that his and Aunt Sue's dutiful conversation made both of them squirm. She liked him but found his small talk stilted, and I thought I knew why.

Harold is tall, with muscles, but he has a narrow face and a rather long nose and bright gray eyes which make him look eager, and I think people expect him to brighten their lives by showing his enthusiasm for everything. But he isn't like that—he's shy and awkward, especially with older adults, and not usually very talkative. People like him well enough—they can see he's a nice person and that he's not dumb—but when they expect to be all cheered up, they go away from him disappointed in a vague sort of way and without exactly knowing why.

We walked to the Rathole, a large, clean cafe officially named James' Inn after the owner but never called anything but the Rathole by our high school crowd. It was a familiar walk for me, past the bus stop (where the fast, frequent busses made it to the center of downtown in twenty minutes) and the school which I'll never miss although it was all right in its time—I like to keep looking ahead instead of back—and the red brick Methodist church where Aunt Sue and I went almost every Sunday. I'd always rather liked attending, but this last year or so it had begun to bore me and my mind wandered like mad during the services. I didn't plan to go to church any more when I left here, if I did leave, but I couldn't see any point in fussing with Aunt Sue about it before then.

I mean, I believe in God and I don't feel that this has to be logical, but it's an abstraction with me—it's like it doesn't really make any difference if I believe or not as far as how I live my life is concerned. Either way, I'd still try to be an okay person, and believing doesn't help me to be any better. I guess what it does is help me to feel *safer.*

"You're real quiet tonight, Gay," Harold said. "You with it?"

"With it and for it," I answered, responding to an old joke between us that had started a couple of years ago when we'd first begun dating. I couldn't remember the joke now, only the formula, but I suppose that Harold remembered, as he is inclined to sentiment.

I did remember our first date, though, because that night we began the practice that eventually won us the Junior Chamber of Commerce roller skating derby, and I still have the engraved silver cup sitting on my dresser. I had liked another boy, several others, actually, a lot more than Harold, but I chose him as my partner because he was far and away the best skater in school, and for some reason I wanted that cup more than anything.

Of course he was the one who won it—there were at least three other girls in the contest who were much better than I was, but none of the boys could begin to match Harold, and he carried us through to first place and even managed to make me look pretty good while he was at it.

And then he'd insisted that I keep the trophy. I admit that I didn't protest too violently, but for weeks afterward whenever I looked at it gleaming away on *my* dresser I felt a little guilty, and that's why I went out with him about half the times he asked during that period. Then I got used to the trophy, but also to Harold, who'd become a kind of convenient habit. I dated quite a few other boys, too—movies, bowling, parties—but always went to dances with Harold as he danced as well as he skated.

Then after the senior prom, he'd asked me if I'd come to his house for dinner that Sunday and meet his family. He'd mentioned it casually enough, but I knew that in his mind that was practically the same thing as getting engaged, and I refused fairly abruptly and hadn't gone out with him since until tonight.

"Listen, Harold," I said, "why don't you take that cup?"

"Cup?" We had reached the Rathole and he stood by the door, blinking at me. "You mean that skating cup?"

I nodded. "It's really yours."

"Yours, too." And he sort of muttered, "What do you think I am, an Indian giver?"

"I've had it long enough." This was certainly true, I thought, and I hadn't really looked at it for months.

"Forget it." He pushed at the door.

"Your mother might like it."

"My mother?" He blinked again. "Aw, cut it out, Gay."

"Okay. Just let me know if you change your mind."

The Rathole was crowded but Mr. James beckoned to us and led us to a table with a reserved card on it. "We didn't make a reservation," Harold told him.

"Who does?" Mr. James spread out his hands and grinned. "But I've got to look out for my special friends."

"Us big spenders," Harold said, and we all laughed. He mowed the James' grass and weeded their garden and I baby sat at least once a week with their three—I hate to say it but it's so true—little brats, and since we both did good jobs and showed up on time, Mr. James always fussed over us a little and delivered the first pair of cokes in person and on the house.

Harold put some quarters in the juke box and we

danced a couple of times, but I simply went through the motions without really feeling the beat. I was already bored and wanted only to be alone so that I could think about Sandy.

"As soon as Velma shows, we'll take off," Harold said as we maneuvered our way back to the table.

"Velma?" I hadn't known we were double-dating, but I was glad that Velma would be around to keep the conversation going.

"She met a new guy somewhere and he belongs to a kind of a club over on the north side of town and we've got it fixed up to go over there tonight." His bright squirrel eyes seemed to promise excitement. "That's the surprise."

"What kind of a club?"

"Psychedelic. It's called the Hanging Eye."

"Good grief."

"Same to you." Velma moved up from behind me, laughing. "Hinge up your jaw, doll. You know I love to sneak up on people." She turned and I saw her date. I don't know why—he was average looking and his clothes were okay and he hadn't said a word yet—but the first thought that came to my mind about him was "hood." And he was old—at least thirty. There were lines at the sides of his eyes.

"Gay, Ray," Velma said and giggled, pointing to me. "*This* is Gay. *You're* not gay, are you, Ray?"

"Hell, no." His mouth smiled but his eyes bored right into me. He more or less gave me the creeps and if Harold wasn't so big and loaded with muscle, I'd never have set foot out of the Rathole with that character along.

"And you remember Harold." While they shook hands, Velma whispered to me, "I picked him up, can you imagine? *Picked him up.*"

Well, what was I supposed to do—send up a flare? The point she was getting across, of course, was that *I* would never be able to pull off a stunt like that, but Velma thought she knew more about me than she actually did.

Oh, if she only knew who *I* had found!

"In a drugstore, of all places." Velma was obviously disappointed at my reaction, or lack of one, and she finished kind of lamely. "Downtown, last week-end."

She added, close to my ear, "He was buying safeties—I saw them," and I knew she was lying because even Velma would not pick up someone right after she saw him buy those.

"No use hanging around here." Ray's glance sneered around the room.

"Not when the Eye—" Velma began but Ray the Hood clapped his hand over her mouth.

"I've heard all the damned puns I can take on that one." And he sort of bumped her (very suggestively) out of the Rathole while she pretended to be scared to death and Harold and I tagged along behind.

His car was a '72 Chevy and didn't seem like anything special to me, but Harold looked it over appreciatively and then asked, "She fixed?"

"Yeah."

"Fifteen seconds?"

Ray smirked. "Thirteen."

Harold nodded, impressed but trying to seem cool.

I'd heard Harold talk enough about speeds to know that he was asking if the car could start out cold and do a quarter-mile in fifteen seconds, but I still wasn't terribly interested.

For most of the way to the club they talked cars, hardly letting Velma get a word in edgewise, and then Harold told us about the car he was going to buy. I barely listened as I'd heard it all dozens of times before and I remember thinking sarcastically that if he ever did really buy that car we would have to christen it in high style. A bottle of champagne broken over its bumper would seem downright prosaic. No, that particular car-warming would have to be a momentous event that would reverberate through history.

Oh, God, the thoughts we think and the predictions we make without thinking. If I'd known then how my own history was shaping up I'd have leaped from the car right then, fast as Ray was driving, and run all the way home and hidden myself in the cellar.

But at that moment, christening Harold's future car was only an idle thought on a dreary drive.

We had to open a wrought iron gate, walk down some dirty cement steps and go through a violent red door before we were finally in the Hanging Eye. The room was fairly dark and Harold and I stood there staring and blinking at the weird colored shapes projected onto the walls—purple silhouettes of women with six legs, white circles changing into pink triangles, and so on.

Velma whispered right into my ear. "It's all fixed up like the sixties, honest. It's like what kids our age liked when you and I were just being born." She laughed softly. "Old hippies never die."

Ray led us to a table almost directly under the huge plastic eye ball that hung from the ceiling. The iris was piebald and the white part was streaked with red, like a map, and had names of towns, Dullsville and Love and Goliath, printed here and there, in bright green.

Harold said he was going to paint his car like that girl's face and Velma asked if he meant the one with the psychedelic make-up or the one with the tattoos. Either way, she said, his choice wasn't exactly limited. He could have spots, blobs, stripes, streaks, smears, or even belly buttons.

"Shut up and look," Ray told her as a swirl of multi-colored rings swept over the walls, giving a kind of insane world within a world within a world effect.

Two muscular boys wearing sequined trunks and slabs of green eye shadow got up to talk-sing and a color wheel revolved to spotlight them first in green, then in red, orange, purple, yellow, and blue. Slowly, so that we could follow the colors, and then picking up speed so that I got a little dizzy and remembered when I was ten and Rennie six and we would look up at a ceiling light and turn around and around and have giggling fits.

Everyone applauded wildly when the boys bowed. "Clap," Ray said, and I noticed that his mouth was thin and sharp, like a weapon. I clapped before I thought and then was annoyed with myself for obeying him so fast and automatically.

It was worse when he grinned, showing me that he knew how I felt and why, so when he said, "Dance?" I answered shortly, "No" and then felt better when his grin disappeared.

"*I'll* dance with you," Velma said, on her feet while Ray the Hood sat there sulking and not even looking at her. Velma turned to Harold. "Will *you* dance with me?"

"Sure, I guess so." He looked at me but I shrugged. I could have been more gracious but who wants to make a big point out of something like that?

"Thought we'd never get a second alone." Ray wasn't smiling and his eyes looked into mine but his tone was pleasant. "Don't bug me, doll. I'm planning big things for you."

"Like pot?" I said. "Or bananas?"

"Well, well." He still wasn't smiling. "Maybe you're not as innocent as you look?" His razor mouth twisted. "Or do you just know a couple of words?"

"I'll bet you like a girl with spirit," I said flatly, hating him.

"Ah, don't be like that." Grinning now, he asked, "What're you doing with that big ape?"

"You mean Harold?" I honestly had thought they had got along quite well.

He laughed. "Forget him. Listen, Gay, how do you like this place?"

I looked at the luminous paint doodles and the ultraviolet bulbs to light them, although the paintings, as Omar might say, were weird enow. I saw the spotlights playing for patterns and movement and the people sitting and staring at them, trying to turn on. "It would have achieved about the same effect," I said, "and been a lot less trouble, to use a few fun-house mirrors."

A waitress with ketchup-colored talon fingernails asked us what we'd have. Ray waved her away and stood up. "We'll move in the other room so we can get some juice." He saw me glancing toward the dance area and muttered, "They'll find us — c'mon."

Banana plants in hookahs. Giant buttons on the walls.

"You're pretty psychedelectable, baby."

Ignoring this, I read the button slogans: Is there LIFE after BIRTH? Save water—shower with a friend.

"You need a real experience."

I thought of dirty bare mattresses and smoking grass and swallowing pills and playing with snakes and smelling colors, and I read another slogan: UFOS are real—the Air Force is a Myth.

"We'd get you ready first," Ray said. "And I'd stay with you for the whole trip."

Now what—a joke about passing the acid test? "That old stuff," I said.

He glared at me. "It's still around, babe," he muttered. "Don't kid yourself. It isn't all snort and sniff. Let me show you the real world."

The next button advised: STAMP OUT REALITY.

Velma and Harold found us and the girl with the bloody claws took our orders. I wasn't used to drinking anything but an occasional glass of Aunt Sue's homemade wine so I had coffee and the smell of it was wonderful. It offset the odor of cheap incense which we were probably supposed to think was marijuana. You had to give A for effort at the Hanging Eye.

Harold told us about his job for the summer as an attendant at Twin Elms Villa, a privately owned hospital for mental patients at the southern tip of the city. "You'd never guess how steep the rates are by what they pay the help," he said ruefully, "but I figure by September I'll have enough for the car."

The car again. I tuned out, remembering our senior class fieldtrip to the state psychiatric hospital. One patient, a huge woman who wore an old purple bathrobe as if it was ermine and a towel around her head as if it was a tiara, swept past us and nodded imperiously to us, her subjects.

I heard one of the patients tell another one, "If you don't stop that clearing your throat you're going to drive me crazy." I remember giggling and then pretending that I was coughing, but I saw the one who had spoken glare at me and knew that I hadn't fooled her. I was truly sorry about that.

There were a few shouting, aggressive patients, but most of them just seemed to sit around with their heads in their hands, very sad. It was all very depressing and I couldn't get those people off my mind for days afterwards. I felt that I'd rather die than ever be an inmate there.

I've always had some fairly odd thoughts, and that visit prompted me to read some books on mental illness to try to learn a little more about myself. I found out that I wasn't anything like those patients. That is, I am *somewhat* like them because we *all* are, but I was a lot more different than I'd secretly expected to be.

I'm not really very strange at all. I don't even have deja-vu.

"How about joining us this round, Gay?" Ray signalled to a pale, skinny waitress who looked like a ghost. I shook my head and he looked at me mockingly. "Can't stand the action?"

"Too true," I admitted coolly.

"Never juice up at all?"

"Only on Aunt Sue's wine."

"The saints preserve us!" Velma rolled her eyes. "Auntie Sue." Trying to impress Ray, she pursed her lips thoughtfully. "Well, that's not quite as bad as Aunt Min, is it, or Aunt Em? Or how about Aunt Bea?"

Velma really wants everybody to like her, but sometimes she goes about it in exactly the wrong way.

Ray stayed poker-faced, staring at me, but Harold frowned and said, "Cut it out, Velma," and she decided to have coffee, too, and then didn't say another word for five minutes. I really think she could get to like Harold quite a lot if he would give her a chance.

He talked about the advanced auto mechanics course he was going to take in the fall and how he would learn diesel after that and get paid, too. "A couple of years and I'll be set with a good profession."

It hardly sounded like a profession to me, but of course I didn't say so. It was a good trade and he would be happy in it and earn a good living. Great. Some people have their lives all planned, with every move, practically, mapped out. This amazes me and makes me feel envious because I honestly don't know what I'll be doing a month from now, don't even know what's going to happen to me from one minute to the next.

The pale girl materialized with our drinks. Velma sipped away at her coffee, Ray looked bored, and Harold had talked himself out, so I said, "Speaking of jobs—" and sighed. "Velma and I start ours Monday." Only Harold looked interested. "Anderson's Insurance in Eastwood. We'll be clerk-typists. Oh, well, it's a change from baby sitting."

Ray sneered a little but didn't say anything. Jobs were for squares. Nobody had to say it.

Harold and I got up to dance. The floor was crowded

and there was a lot of noise. Everything was lights and movement and color, and yet it was all so drab!

I thought of Sandy's mature quietness and of the fascination of this contrasted with his colorful appearance —the black hair and eyes, tanned skin and rosy lips. And with all the muscles flexed around me, the memory of his slender, naked back was somehow touching.

"Ray gave me a guest card," Harold said, "so we could come back here sometime, if you wanted to."

"He's a troll."

"Sure, he is. Who's asking *him*?"

I shrugged, not intending to go out with Harold again. It would be pointless. He couldn't mean anything to me even if I hadn't met Sandy.

Sandy. He was too good to be true. Would I really see him tomorrow? Would he really show up?

The evening sort of wore on. Velma and Harold were enjoying the new atmosphere and of course it was Ray's *home*, but it had palled pretty fast for me, although I probably would have been more interested if I hadn't kept thinking of Sandy.

We saw one of our former teachers across the room and even from that distance we could hear his high, campy voice as he let his hair down with his friends. I must have stared because Ray said, "What's the matter, baby? Can't tell the hes from the shes?"

"Of course I can," I snapped, irritated because I'd been confused in exactly that way twice in the last hour.

"Then you're a better man than I am," he quipped and grinned heartily at his own cleverness. Under Velma's covering laughter, he leaned over and muttered, "You can always find me here."

As if I hadn't known. As if I cared.

Velma asked me if I wanted to powder my nose and what can you ever say when the other girl asks that? I mean, you get up and go whether you want to or not. I knew she was dying to tell me something and once inside, she let her excitement show. Nothing could keep Velma down for long.

"Did you see him?"

"You mean Mr. Barton?"

"Uh huh! He's quit teaching, Ray said. He's working in some faggot art shop downtown."

"How come Ray knows so much about him?"

"He *blackmailed* him! He told me so." This was her big news. "Most of last year, I guess, and then Mr. B. resigned."

"Well, that's pretty rotten." When Velma laughed I felt defensive and tried to explain. "It's like stabbing a cat for catching a mouse."

"Make sense, will you?" She looked in the mirror above the sink and put on another layer of lipstick.

"I mean, it's only doing what it's geared to do."

Velma laughed again and blotted her mouth with a piece of toilet paper. "He's geared, all right."

I followed her out and stopped when she did at Mr. Barton's table. He and the three young men with him stood up and returned her friendly greeting.

"We'll miss you at school next year," Velma said, even though she had graduated with me the week before and certainly had no intention of going back.

"Why, thank you." Mr. Barton's voice was normal again, to my relief. "I'll miss the students, too, of course."

I felt sorry for him as he had really tried to get economics across to us in an interesting way and had never played favorites.

"But I'm happy with my new work," he added after a little pause.

Velma should have left it like that, but she was hurt and angry and had to strike back. She'd had this big crush on Mr. Barton all last year and then found out he liked boys. "You were always so good at answering questions," she said. "Maybe you could give me some advice now."

"Sure. I can try, anyway."

"Well, this woman keeps following me." Velma didn't bother to lower her voice and people at near-by tables looked up at her and waited. "She backs me into corners and rubs my arms. Like this." She demonstrated. I stood there paralyzed with embarrassment. I seemed to be rooted to the spot. "I thought maybe you could tell me what to do."

Mr. Barton managed a smile but his eyes wavered. "I'd mention it to my parents, if I were you."

"Oh." Velma widened her eyes. "Don't you approve of that sort of carrying on?"

Someone at the next table snickered, and I came to and took Velma's arm and pulled her away. One of Mr. Barton's friends said softly, "She seems to know how to work off her aggressions."

Walking back to our table, I growled at Velma. "Somebody ought to splatter you all over the wall." But I knew that it must be pretty devastating to feel a lot of emotion for someone who not only didn't but *couldn't* feel anything for her. "Why don't you lay off?"

Velma never wants either pity or criticism and she answered very flippantly. "Because maybe he's ambisextrous." She shrugged my hand off her arm and then winked to show me that she wasn't really humiliated, just playing it for laughs. "AC-DC, you dig? Maybe I'm still in the running."

"You've got a fat chance."

Before she sat down she stuck out her tongue at me, and grinned.

I smiled back but my eyes smarted in the smoky room and my head began to ache.

Ray tried to play footsies under the table.

I'd really had enough of the Hanging Eye, and it was midnight. I asked if we could leave.

Velma wanted to stay on a while, and I knew she was O.K. now, so Harold and I took a bus downtown and then transferred to our east side bus. "We can go back there by ourselves," Harold said when we reached my house. "It'll be more fun without them. I'll call you."

"No." I shook my head. "I don't like the place."

"Well, what *would* your majesty like?"

I wasn't thinking of him. I was thinking of Sandy, but I can see Harold even now, standing on the front porch, frowning in irritation and disappointment. And I knew I was making him feel worse when he bent down to kiss me goodnight and I turned my face so that his lips only dampened my cheek.

3

By ten o'clock I was dressed for my date with Sandy. I had begun getting ready at eight-thirty. Usually, fifteen or twenty minutes is time enough to put on clothes and make-up, but this was so very special and important that I got nervous and kept doing everything wrong. My hand trembled and smeared my lipstick, for example, and I had to do the whole job over three times. And I wouldn't ordinarily wear lipstick at all. I couldn't decide whether to brush my hair from left to right or from right to left or whether I should wear flats or medium heels, even though ordinarily I wouldn't waste a second on such minor decisions. It seemed to take a long time to pull myself together and *relate* to things, as I was excited and dreamy at the same time and never once that morning altogether sane.

I have two "best" cotton dresses, one pink and one blue, and I thought I would go out of my mind trying to decide which one to wear. I finally chose the blue, which is just a little fancier with its pleated bodice, and then added a touch of costume jewelry—a pearl necklace and matching earrings—to make me look a little older. The total effect was pretty good, I thought.

When Aunt Sue saw me, she said, "Oh, all dressed up. A date?"

"Mm hmm." I marveled at my steady voice, admired my firm hand as I poured myself a cup of coffee, and was absolutely awed by my unfaltering legs as I walked to the table and sat down.

"Harold again?" Aunt Sue had washed the breakfast dishes and was drying the last of them, a job I should have done and would have done if I hadn't taken so long with my frantic primping. "I was beginning to wonder if he'd moved away or something, and now he shows up twice in a row." She didn't seem to expect an answer and, although I knew it was high time to speak up, I sat there in silence.

I told myself that if Aunt Sue could meet Sandy before she heard my story, she would be more receptive to it. I was feverishly nervous, really, about seeing him again, unsure of what to say or do, and I knew that waiting until he came to tell Aunt Sue would only add to the confusion and awkwardness. And yet I couldn't seem to find the right words to explain.

A pick-up in the woods. To Aunt Sue it would sound so much worse than it had been. I could say that we had met through friends at the library, but I doubted that Sandy would want to go along with a made-up story, and I was not sure that I would want this, either. I felt that Sandy and I were going to be important to each other and I didn't want to start out with a lie. But I was really not looking forward to telling Aunt Sue how I had met him.

Not that she is intolerant—she's been very understanding about my impulsiveness and my crushes in school and cooperative about my dating. But she is close to fifty, for one thing, and also she's never been married—I think because she was never *particularly* drawn to men and hadn't ever felt that her happiness depended on one special man—and so our attitudes have to be different. Aunt Sue and I are very close and at the same time worlds apart.

I suppose that no matter how attached we are to another person, we are still alone. Sometimes I really feel lonely, and a few times I have even picked up hitchhikers just to have someone to talk to. (The last one was a Ray the Hood type and nothing happened but he made me quite nervous.) I have friends—Velma and Harold and others—but it's like I'm searching for someone else, or something else.

If I tried to explain this feeling to Aunt Sue, she would be all worried and end up by stuffing me with vitamin pills and sending me over to Dr. Horseley's office for a shot.

I know that Aunt Sue cares a lot about me and that she's there backing me, but she does expect me to make my own bed and then lie in it. Yet, knowing that we must be independent, and even wanting to be, we still keep looking for someone so that we won't be alone. At least I do.

So, different as we are, I can't tell Aunt Sue everything. I wouldn't want to hurt her feelings or make her angry if I could help it, although of course I've done both in the last four or five years. And she's annoyed me a few times, too, but when I get mad I kick an old tire I keep under my bed. This usually, even if not always, keeps me from yelling at Aunt Sue and makes life more pleasant for both of us.

If she knew about the hitchhikers she would explode, and I don't think she has a tire under her bed. I didn't know how she would react to hearing about the way I had met Sandy. It wasn't that I was afraid of what she would *do*, but I worried about how she would *feel*.

I waited in the kitchen without telling her, waited with my hands damp and sticky around the coffee cup, listening for the sound of the Jaguar's motor, wishing first that Sandy would hurry and then that he would not, and finally, as eleven o'clock came and went, wanting to burst into tears at the thought that he was not going to show up at all.

At eleven-thirty, when I was ready to scream with tension, Aunt Sue calmly announced that if she didn't hurry she would be late for her lunch date.

"Lunch date?" I wondered what she was talking about.

"Why, yes, with Flo Bonner." She gave me an odd glance. "I told you not an hour ago. And why do you suppose I changed into my good suit?"

I hadn't heard, hadn't even noticed that Aunt Sue had left the kitchen and returned. Nothing had registered but my own inner churning. "You look great," I said and she smiled and went out the door, waving when I called after her, "Have a nice time and say hello to Mrs. Bonner for me."

I put my head in my arms on the table and gave up hoping for Sandy to come. I tried to resign myself to a whole world of shattered dreams.

A few minutes later I heard the sound of Sandy's car and for a moment I froze. Then I leaped from the chair and ran into my room and looked at myself in the mirror.

My nose wasn't shiny but I dabbed some powder on it anyway, picked up both my comb and lipstick and put them down again. It was the glitter in my eyes that needed disguising, and I couldn't do anything about that.

I ran to open the front door and reached it just as Sandy pressed the bell. "Hello, Gay."

"Hi." I felt very shy in spite of his bright smile. "Hi, Sandy."

Neither of us said anything more but walked together to his car. I watched his profile as he drove. He offered no explanation for his lateness and didn't even mention it. I was puzzled, but I was sure that he would not be deliberately rude and so I decided that time simply meant very little to him. I know that some people feel that way about time and I decided not to say a word, even in a joking tone, to Sandy about his arriving at twenty to twelve when our date was for ten. I was grateful that he had come at all.

He didn't seem to notice that I said very little as we rode through town. He seemed to be concentrating on his driving and he looked quite relieved when he parked. "This is where I live," he said, nodding toward a large and very intimidating stone apartment building. "We had a country house when my father was alive, but now Mother prefers to be in the center of things."

So he lived with his mother. "It's more convenient in the city," I said, making conversation, "if she likes shopping and —"

But Sandy was already out of the car and opening the door on my side. "She's waiting to meet you, Gay."

"Your *mother*?" The thought chilled me. I mean, I didn't even know Sandy yet, at least not well enough to feel secure, and I was afraid of meeting his mother. I had a mental picture of a huge, haughty woman in a black gown with a diamond brooch, looking down her nose at me through her lorgnette.

Wildly, I thought of saying that I was in the middle of a heart attack, but Sandy said, "You'll like her, Gay," and took my arm to help me out of the car.

And she'll be crazy about me, too, I thought drearily, walking with Sandy past the uniformed doorman into the lobby and toward the elevator.

"Did you tell her about us?" I asked with little hope. "About how we met?"

"Yes."

Oh God, I thought.

We got off at the top floor and Mrs. Carlyle let us into the apartment. Staring at her dark good looks, I hardly heard Sandy's introduction and instead of "How do you do," I blurted, "Why, you're lovely!"

Of course I felt hopelessly awkward then, but she smiled and said graciously, "Thank you, dear. I was just about to say the same thing to you. Do come into the living room, won't you?"

I had thought that we were there. The carpeted, furnished entry hall seemed to me to be a very nice living room, as large as Aunt Sue's and a thousand times more attractive. If Sandy or his mother noticed my confusion, neither of them showed it by so much as a raised eyebrow, and I followed Mrs. Carlyle into the real living room.

"Good heavens!" The room was tremendously beautiful; a fitting place, I thought, for these two handsome people. I felt surrounded by beauty.

"They *are* striking, aren't they?" Mrs. Carlyle touched my arm to guide me toward one of the paintings on the far wall. I hadn't actually noticed individual things, only the total, wondrous effect of the room, but now I studied each painting in turn as the three of us moved from one to the other. There were four, all done in oils, all abstractions and so impressive that I could have spent days looking at each. But one of them especially held my attention because its colors and shapes were so compelling and harmonious and seemed to represent an ideal world. And yet it made me feel that this world was attainable.

"It isn't *quite* perfect, is it, Gay?" Mrs. Carlyle said. "And so you feel that it is real and warm."

"Yes, yes, that's it exactly." I was excited about it and about sharing my thoughts of it with her, and I groped for the right words to offer her. "It—it isn't *marred* by perfection."

Her arm went quickly around my shoulder. She could be impulsive, too, I thought, human, and vulnerable, and not frightening at all.

"This one is Sandy's favorite, too," she said. "But you

must see the others, in his studio."

I think I had known, somehow, that Sandy was the artist. I looked up at him, feeling awed and humble. He smiled. "While Mother shows you around, I think I'll see how Cook is coming with our lunch."

It was an effort not to watch him walk away. My eyes automatically began to follow him and as I forced myself to look around the room, the first thing I saw was the baby grand. "Do you play the piano?" I asked Mrs. Carlyle.

"I'm afraid not," she said ruefully. "Sandy has all the talent in the family." She broke off with another rueful smile. "Oh, Gay, I apologize for talking like such a fond mother. I'm glad Sandy didn't hear me boasting about him."

"He's so—accomplished," I said, so overwhelmed by him, by her, by the glory around me that I felt a little dizzy, and I was grateful that the first stop on our tour was the terrace where I took deep breaths of cool air before admiring the view, which gave me a truly new idea of the city, and the tiny, pampered, exquisite rose garden.

Mrs. Carlyle stooped to pull a weed and watching her, I realized just at that moment that I was overdressed. She was elegant in a simple, unpretentious way and I had tried too hard, had let it show that I cared too much.

Sandy found us in his studio. "I hope there's about half as much food as there was yesterday," I told him, looking at the hamper he carried, "because the squirrels are already spoiled."

Mrs. Carlyle laughed. "As Sandy is by Cook, I'm afraid." She added, "I did want you to lunch with me today, but it would be a shame to postpone a picnic on a day like this. Will you come one day next week?"

"I'd love to," I told her.

"Good." She smiled. "And your aunt, too? I'll be in touch with her."

On the way to the woods, I tried to imagine the

meeting between Aunt Sue and Mrs. Carlyle. Aunt Sue is wonderful, of course, but she *is* kind of drab and not exactly an intellectual. Then, too, the hospitality would have to be returned and oh God, our place after the Carlyles'!

On the other hand, I thought cynically, Mrs. Carlyle was bound to like Aunt Sue because they were both about the same age and Aunt Sue was not nearly as good looking.

Our picnic lunch was delicious. Even Sandy said, "Cook outdid herself today."

"It's wonderful," I agreed. "Real rich." I didn't know what some of the food was, but I was too proud or shy—too much of a snob, really—to ask Sandy, so I ate it in ignorance. And of course there was far too much of it. Even the squirrels could not finish it all.

"I can't get used to your calling the cook Cook," I told Sandy. "It's like naming a pet dog Dog instead of Spot or calling a friend Friend instead of Mary." He smiled and because I wanted to know all about him, I asked, "Did you begin calling her Cook when you were little?"

I waited for him to answer, but he seemed preoccupied, and after quite a long pause, he said suddenly, "You saw me from the highway."

"Why—yes. Yesterday, I did."

"We should move farther back, then. I like privacy."

"All right." I started to gather up our things.

"Not now," he said. "Next time."

I sat back. "Okay. We'll find another place with good tree spacing and maybe we can put up your hammock." Next time, he had said. They were the two sweetest words in the English language.

"Hammock?" He frowned.

"You were measuring the distance between trees," I reminded, "to see if a hammock would fit."

He looked at me blankly for a long moment and then

shrugged and began to strum his guitar. I knew that he had completely forgotten any mention of the hammock and this puzzled me, but as I listened to him play, I forgot about it, too.

"I wish I had a special talent," I told him when the song was finished and he put the guitar aside. "Oh, I don't mean like *yours*, Sandy. Good night, I wouldn't dream of raising my sights *that* high, but, well, I mean talents like some of the kids I knew in school have. Like Jim Wheeler can draw anything from a jeep to a pig and you'd think the jeep could go and the pig could squeal. And Jen McAffrey plays pop piano by ear. Her twin brother Jed is terrific at math. Clay Bell makes furniture and a lot of it is good enough to sell in a store, and Ope designs and sews very nicely. And even Harold is a whiz on skates. Roller or ice, he can't be beat. It's like he had magic in his feet, the way he maneuvers and cavorts and *flies* around the rinks. He's so skillful and graceful that it's a thrill to skate with him!" I laughed a little and Sandy smiled as I added, "Never mind how he bumbles once he takes off the skates.

"So," I went on, "I'm one of those without a special talent. I wish I could sing, for example. I've got one of these contraltos that music teachers put in choruses and never have solo."

Sandy was listening closely and, encouraged by his attention, I kept on talking. "The only thing I've ever done above and beyond the common herd, I guess, is to be a ham radio operator. I had a lot of help, though, or I never would have made it."

"Tell me about it," Sandy said, as if he really wanted to know.

"Well, this was last year, Sandy, when a radio amateur stayed at Aunt Sue's." I thought about Roger's nice, homely face and his crew-cut red hair and his habit of chewing on the ends of all the pencils he used. "He wrote articles for popular science magazines, mostly short pieces about how to build experimental equipment, and he only got about fifty dollars for each one, so he had to keep busy and turn out a lot of them to pay for his food and room and clothes and his monkey, as he called it, which was hamming.

"Anyway, I saved him time by typing his articles, which he scrawled on big yellow sheets of paper and left scattered around for me to decipher. To pay back the favor, he taught me the Morse code and lent me a manual to study. Then he gave me the novice test which I just barely passed, both the five words per minute code test and the written part that I had only memorized without understanding anything much."

I stopped, aware that I was talking quite a lot, and about myself, too, but Sandy nodded for me to go on. He was the first person I'd ever known who really *listened* to me. He seemed to be concentrating on every word I said, and I felt that he was sincerely interested in knowing me.

"Well, now I had my novice license, Roger said, and it was good for a year so I could relax a little and start learning how to be a ham. But he apologized for doing it this way—he knew that it would have been better for me if I had *earned* my ticket—but he didn't know just when he'd be shoving off and he'd wanted me to get a start before he left. From now on, he said, when he could find the time, he'd teach me about the equipment and theory, since I ought to know this to get my general's license.

"But he never found the time and I never learned much more. This was mostly my own fault, though, because I didn't try to learn on my own. I just had fun using his rig to tap out my little messages like 'You are my first Arizona, Bob. How's the weather?' Then the answer would be 'Fine business, Gay. Glad to be your first Arizona. I have three Pennsylvanias but you are my first young lady. Weather is dry here. How is it there?'

"I had cards printed with my call in big red letters and sent one out to everybody I contacted. Most of them answered, and I had cards from seventeen different states before Roger left."

"Send me one," Sandy said. "Pretend you've contacted me."

"Okay." I picked up my purse then, rummaged through it, and tossed it aside. "I was going to show you how the copy goes, but I guess I don't have a pencil and paper."

"Here, use this." Sandy handed me his sketch book and charcoal stick.

I hesitated, touching the thick white pages. "Your good drawing paper?"

"Sure, why not?" He smiled, and I felt a little weak—I guess because his teeth were so white. "This is important."

I wrote "u r my 1st Ariz Bob Hw is the wx?
               F B Gay Glad to be ur 1st Ariz I hv 3 Penn
               but u r my 1st Y L."

"All females are young ladies and all males are old men in Hamland," I explained. "Y Ls and O Ms."

"Very gallant of the OMs," Sandy said, and we laughed.

"When Roger left, he said he was going to have to find time for YLs again," I remembered aloud. "He said that they used to be his habit and he kicked it, but hamming got to be his monkey, too, so he might just as well go back to girls. He said that they were prettier than transmitters, but I don't think he gave up radio for girls. He may have given up writing articles or even eating regularly, but not electronics. He had too much ability."

"I think it's wonderful, your being a ham, Gay," Sandy said. "I really do."

I could feel myself blushing, pleased at his approval but feeling guilty for getting credit I didn't deserve. "I had all that help and it was just a novice class ticket, so it wasn't anything wonderful."

"It was a good beginning."

"Yes, that's just it, Sandy. If I'd gone on by myself and got a general's and put my own rig together, then I'd have something to be proud of."

"Perhaps one day you'll do all that," he said. "In the meantime you've been learning other things, haven't you? We can take in only so much at a time, you know."

I felt better after he said that, but I looked at him and worried about how long a nobody like me could possibly hold his interest. Other people, if they were lucky, had talent, but Sandy had genius.

"I'll teach you to paint, if you like."

"Would you?" I looked at him closely although I knew that he wouldn't say anything he didn't mean. "Are you serious?"

"Sure." His hand touched mine for a second. "I'll bring the materials tomorrow."

"But I can't draw a straight line."

"Why should you? If you ever need a straight line, use a ruler."

He wasn't smiling and I didn't know if he intended that as a joke or not. "I meant I couldn't draw very well. My horses look like cows and my cows like sheep, and —"

"You can learn to draw, Gay," he said, "and you should, but I don't think that's as important as a feeling for form and color, and I'm sure you have this in you to develop."

"Oh, Sandy, do you think so?"

"Yes. You have both warmth and control."

"Oh, Sandy." A herd of stallions galloped inside me. It was his first compliment to me, the first I could claim—at least he made me feel that I could—and what a beauty! For the first time I felt that I might be—oh, not his equal—but almost worthy of him.

I was so much under his spell that if he had asked me to do the lowest, most menial task, I'd have considered it an honor and a privilege.

Or he could have make love to me then and there. But he did not.

4

When I woke up the next morning the first thing I saw was the white curtain fluttering a little in the breeze and I thought, oh, good, it will be a nice day for our picnic, warm but enough wind for comfort.

I wanted to think about Sandy and deliberately postponed doing it, wanting even more to look forward a while longer to the pleasure of thinking of him. I looked around the room, at the powder blue walls, and thought, wouldn't I love to have one of Sandy's paintings hanging there.

This was no way to keep from daydreaming about him, of course. The powder blue walls — red is the color I like best, but I'm too light—too nondescript, really—to wear it. I show up better with pastels, especially blue. But I do use touches of red in my room. Not in big areas like the bedspread (medium blue with a white dust ruffle) or a chair, but in a Pirates' pennant over my desk and a pincushion and an old Halloween devil mask that Rennie used to wear.

My room had always pleased me—I had always been allowed to fix it up any way I liked—but now I couldn't help comparing it with Sandy's. His was three times as large, much more richly furnished, and had its own bath. Even his studio was more elaborate than my room.

Oh, well, I thought, my room is cozy and it suits me to

a T. And this was also no way not to think about Sandy. I'd be better off planning my little speech to Aunt Sue. "I drove by this woods, you see, and there was this faun —" No. I would have to do better than that.

Aunt Sue might say that he was too rich for my blood, but I supposed I would have to answer that he was already in my blood and it was too late for a warning.

I turned on my radio and listened to a little country music. Some of it has a nice beat, but a lot of it is just sentimental soft porn. But I like some of it.... I turned off the radio and thought about Sandy, his rich dark eyes....

I reached for my guitar and began to strum the chords for "Black is the Color of my True Love's Hair." Sometimes I just have to sing that song. The need to sing it hits me and nothing else can satisfy me.

I sang softly, though, because I wanted it to be private and I could hear Aunt Sue moving around in the kitchen.

> *"Oh, I love my love and well he knows;*
> *I love the ground whereon he goes.*
> *If you no more on earth I see*
> *My life will quickly fade away."*

At breakfast, Aunt Sue told me that she'd been almost asleep last night when she saw the bathroom light go on for a second and then go out again. "I knew it wasn't you, Gay," she said, "because I'd've heard you come in."

I have to go through the kitchen and her bedroom to get to the bathroom, and someday in the far future I'm going to have a personal, exclusive bathroom, very modern with a pink tub the size of a small swimming pool, a gadget to heat the towels, wall to wall mirrors and carpeting, toothpaste dispensers, and musical soap dishes that play Beethoven's Fifth. Aunt Sue's bathroom even has an old-fashioned button instead of a switch for the light.

"It went on all by itself," Aunt Sue said conversationally. "Will you have some more toast, Gay?"

There is that about her—she doesn't understand electricity any more than I do, but she knows that wires can be loose and connections not quite right and she doesn't yell "Ghost!" and get hysterical about things.

Also, this is what she is like: One morning she heard me groaning and, naturally, she came hurrying into my room, afraid I was sick. But when I told her that I was okay and just happened to feel like groaning, she only looked at me for a couple of seconds, then smiled a little and said, "All right" and left me to groan in peace.

Now I looked at her watching the slots where the toast would pop up, and I did a kind of double-take, because she was actually pretty. I had never really noticed before, but her face was soft and heart-shaped and her eyes were a deep, lovely shade of blue. She seemed younger than she had yesterday.

I looked away and picked up the cream pitcher. It always makes me want to laugh.

"What's tickling you?" Aunt Sue asked and reached for the toast.

"Have you ever noticed that this pitcher is shaped exactly like a john seat?"

She looked startled for a moment before she laughed and said, "No, but I'm sure I will from now on."

I told her then about Sandy and how I had met him, omitting most of the details. I said it all fairly fast to get it over with and ended by saying, "His mother is going to ask you for lunch or tea or something soon. I know you'll like her. And oh, Aunt Sue, wait till you see their apartment. It's a decorator's dream!"

"Impulsiveness is bound to get you adventures," she said. Her tone was neutral but she frowned a little and rather nervously began to butter the toast all over again.

Sometimes I know when to keep quiet. I waited and

she added, "You say his mother wants to meet me?"

"Mm hmm, she's going to call you soon. And of course you'll meet Sandy today." I tried to speak casually but I wanted to shout with excitement at the thought of him.

Aunt Sue nodded thoughtfully. I don't think she would have said any more then even if Mrs. Unger hadn't tapped on the door just at that moment like a character in a play and, after accepting the invitation to sit down and have some coffee, announced that she would be giving up her room at the end of the week.

"Me and Tokie," she said, "have found us a little apartment on the north side. We need a living room to put Tokie's piano in."

For years Mrs. Alma Unger had talked about the day that her daughter would be old enough to take piano lessons. They had come to live at Aunt Sue's four years ago when Tokie was only three. Mrs. Unger was a huge, positive woman, but Tokie was tiny enough for someone half her age and very shy and nervous. She reminded me of a Chihuahua dog and when people see a hairless, quivering little creature like that they don't know whether to pick it up and cuddle it or kick it away into a corner. So, of course, feeling guilty about a thought like kicking the poor thing, we are always extra special nice to it, and I think that is the main reason all of us in the house babied and fussed over Tokie.

That plus the fact that Mrs. Unger told everyone that Tokie was illegitimate. "I'm sure glad I never got rid of her, though," Mrs. Unger had confided to Aunt Sue and me one day over cocoa in the kitchen. "I mean, you know, before she was born, because she is the sweetest thing going."

I remember that Aunt Sue glanced over at me and I kept my face blank since I wanted to hear the rest of the conversation.

"But I'm waiting till she grows up and we can be real friends, you know? Like when we get settled permanent somewhere I want her to take piano lessons."

Aunt Sue and I looked at each other as people do after a remark that doesn't seem to make sense and Mrs. Unger, catching the glance, said, "What I mean is, for a long time it'll be me nagging at her to practice and her whining about it, see? And I'll say it's culture and art and her soul and all that stuff. 'You'll be glad later,' I'll tell her. Then when she's grown up I can say, 'See, all them lessons and practice paid off. I figured some day you'd want to play piano in a whore house.'"

She laughed until it dawned on her that her audience wasn't with her. "It's an old joke, sure," she explained, "and it'd go over better if Tokie was a *boy*, but it'll seem funny to her *then*, see? I have to wait till she's grown up and we're real friends." She looked at us expectantly.

"I'd appreciate it if you'd wait until *my* girl is grown up, too," Aunt Sue said icily.

"Oh." Mrs. Unger's smile faded. "Uh, well, I'm sorry. I sure am." She looked so uncomfortable that I smiled at her and said truthfully that I hadn't laughed only because I hadn't understood the joke.

"Gay is only thirteen." Aunt Sue, only partly mollified, seemed to be warning her not to explain anything else.

"Thirteen?" Mrs. Unger proceeded to undo the good her apology had done. "Why, shoot, when I was thirteen I could of told you jokes that would curl your —" She stopped talking and grinning to glare back at Aunt Sue, but nobody can outglare Aunt Sue when she is feeling righteously indignant, and Mrs. Unger gave up trying and wheeled around and stomped out of the kitchen. It was the only time I ever saw her even a little angry. We had touched her one sensitive area—Tokie grown up. We heard her say quite loudly in the hall, "Ah, shoot, some people got no sense of humor. If Tokie grows up like that I'll throw her out, piano and all.''

This all makes Mrs. Unger sound stupid and crude, and she was some of each, but she had a special quality about her that Aunt Sue and I mentioned often. She had *warmth*. She responded to everybody with zest and seemed to be saying, ''We're all in this old world together, so what the hell, let's be friends.'' Everybody felt this and was drawn to her as if she was a big, warm, friendly sun.

And strange as it may seem, Mrs. Unger was the one who had given me the first encouragement about going to college. It happens that way sometimes. I mean you get to talking and somebody says sure you can do this job or go on to school or whatever, and you know you can, even if you hadn't thought so before.

So, wrapped up as I was in my dreams of Sandy when Mrs. Unger told us that she and Tokie were leaving, I still felt something like a stone dropping inside me and I knew that I would miss them both.

''We won't be able to move into the apartment for about a month,'' Mrs. Unger was saying, ''but I'm going to take Tokie to Wyoming while we're waiting. We'll hitchhike,'' she added casually.

Aunt Sue reacted the way she was supposed to: ''Hitchhike! All the way to Wyoming? With a seven-year-old child?''

''Why not?'' Mrs. Unger shrugged and beamed. ''I'll take good care of her.''

''Well, of course you will, but —'' Aunt Sue stopped, apparently at a loss for words.

''You took Gay there once when she was little, didn't you?''

''Well, yes, Alma, but Gay was twelve and *we didn't hitchhike.*''

''Aw, shoot.'' Mrs. Unger grinned at me. ''Think what

you missed out on, kid—the experience of a lifetime.''

I couldn't help grinning back—her smile always lit up the whole room—and Aunt Sue smiled, too, before she pointed out that busses were safe.

"Safe, shmafe." Mrs. Unger was having a great time as usual. Aunt Sue was always just shockable enough to be the perfect audience for her. "You think some monster is going to attack us on Interstate 80? Listen, he'll take one look at these —" She flexed her biceps dramatically.

I excused myself and left them to it. I wanted to go downtown, before Sandy came, and try to find something, anything, to make me look better. I don't know what I had in mind but I felt a desperate need for something new and flattering to impress him. As I went out of the kitchen, Aunt Sue said slyly, "He'll take one look at your big rear, too, Alma, and —" The rest of the sentence lost out to Mrs. Unger's appreciative laugh.

In my room, I changed clothes completely, underwear and all, falling carefully into my bra, smoothing my slip, and taking a lot of trouble with my plainer, pink "best" cotton dress and my hair and make-up to achieve a deceptively simple effect, making me look as good as possible but as if I hadn't tried.

Then I rushed downtown and spent an hour trying on wigs to see if a new hair style or color would help, but I didn't see anything that really caught me so I combed my hair and rushed back home just in case Sandy should happen to be on time.

I saw the white Jag parked (crookedly) at the curb and stood still for a moment, panicked. He was here, early this time. My mind seemed to be blank—what would I say to him? He must have met Aunt Sue. I hoped that she had found something to say to him, hoped that the living room did not seem too small and drab to him, hoped that I could walk inside and greet him pleasantly and calmly and get our day together off to a good start.

Sandy and Aunt Sue were sitting at the kitchen table, drinking coffee and talking so cozily that for a minute neither one of them noticed me in the doorway. "I see you two have met," I said, which was trite, of course, but absolutely the only thing I could think of. Sandy in the *kitchen*. Oh, Aunt Sue, I thought, how could you? It was all right, though, everything was all right. Sandy stood up and smiled and when we left Aunt Sue, I drove to the woods and we found a heavenly new place there, out of sight of the highway and with trees just far enough apart for the hammock Sandy had brought.

It was a perfect day altogether—the weather, the food, the setting, and the conversation. Sandy had liked Aunt Sue. "I think she is a very kind person," he said and I nodded, proud of Aunt Sue and grateful to her for pleasing him.

And the hammock was for me. Sandy never did remember mentioning it himself, but he remembered that I had and, thinking that I wanted one, had got it for me. Actually, I hate hammocks—I always manage to fall out of them somehow—but what a nice thing for Sandy to do. What a sweet, sweet thought!

Because the day with Sandy had been so satisfying I couldn't understand why, later at home, I tried to pick a quarrel with Aunt Sue. I began by saying that I would have been happier if she had entertained Sandy in the living room while he waited for me.

"Oh, it just seemed more natural to have him sit down right where the coffee was," Aunt Sue said cheerfully. "He didn't seem to mind."

Then I asked her what she had thought of Sandy. "Did you like him?"

"Oh, yes, he's a nice boy."

"Fine," I said flatly. "A nice boy." I didn't know why I felt so surly all of a sudden. "Is *that* all you can say about *Sandy*?"

"Well, I think he's a lonely young man," she answered mildly, "but I suppose what you want to hear is that he's handsome."

I didn't smile back at her. "And wonderful."

"All right." After a pause she added, "He's very well mannered, too, but I'd say—reserved or, well, not exactly shy, but he keeps himself to himself."

After another silence, I said, "Thanks for not saying it."

"For not saying what?" She looked honestly bewildered.

"That he's too rich for my blood."

Her expression changed to thoughtfulness and then to a kind of teasing smile. "For all I know," she said lightly, "you may be too rich for his."

But I could not match her mood. "Aren't you going to tell me not to get too serious about him?" I demanded, more or less wadding my own frustration into a ball and throwing it at her.

She refused to catch it, though. "Well, I probably would," she answered amiably, "if you hadn't already told yourself so many times."

I was annoyed with myself and so I snapped at her. "Don't you know I'm just a diversion for him and I mustn't expect to see him any more when the summer's over?" I felt like smashing something. "Don't you know I'll meet dozens of other men before I'm twenty and think I'm in love with at least half of them?"

"My goodness," Aunt Sue said. "You seem to have the whole lecture down pat. Now that should save some wear and tear on my vocal cords."

But in spite of her light tone, I was sure that I saw pity in her eyes and I ran to my room and slammed the door behind me and lay on my bed fuming and sulking.

A few moments later I heard a soft tap on the door and Aunt Sue's voice. "Gay? Gay, dear, I'm going to bake some cookies. If you feel like helping—''

If you feel like talking, I'm here if you need me.

I didn't answer, and she went away.

Nothing had changed, really, but I knew she understood and I began to feel a little better somehow. I stayed in my room, lying there alone, sullenly aloof, for an hour or two until most of the misery wore off.

5

When Aunt Sue told me that Opal had called, it made me remember things I hadn't thought of for quite a while. I hadn't seen her for at least a year and a half, but I was sure that she hadn't changed. I didn't think Ope would ever change.

She has these big dark blue eyes and white teeth and yellow hair, and all this dazzles you so you don't catch on for a long time that she isn't really pretty. She's attractive and warm and a little ignorant and the best friend I ever had except for Aunt Sue.

Ope had been staying at Aunt Sue's for over two years by the time Rennie and I came to live there, right after our parents died. I spent the night of my twelfth birthday in the little back room on the second floor, the only one empty when we moved in, and even Rennie hadn't remembered what day it was. He kept saying, "Gay, aren't they ever coming back?" and I had to tell him, "No, Rennie, no, when you die you don't come back. But Mother and Dad both believed in heaven and you can bet that's where they are right now."

"When I grow up," he said, "I'll never drive a car—never."

Aunt Sue tried to make us feel better by saying, "I'm so grateful you two weren't with them," but Rennie said he wasn't grateful at all and he wished he had been in the car with them when they crashed because he would rather be dead than living here without them. Aunt Sue left us alone for a while then and I said, "Rennie, you keep quiet now. You're only nine and don't know everything and you're only making Aunt Sue feel worse. Dad was her brother, remember, and she's got to take care of us now."

He muttered, "She doesn't either have to," and cried some more.

"She wants to," I told him. "There aren't any other relatives for us or for her, either," and looking at him curled up on the bed so miserable, I started to cry, too. When Aunt Sue came back, she cried with us. After a while, she fixed us all some supper which we managed to eat before we cried again. This went on for two days off and on with the three of us making each other feel better even with all the tears, because we were glad we had each other. Then there was the funeral and by that time we were pretty much cried out and only looked sad without breaking down in front of everybody. When we were back again in the house we all cried again, not for the last time but not like before, either.

Ope came to see us later on that day and said she hadn't come before out of respect for our feelings (she had the room next door and had heard us crying a lot). She had been to the funeral. She said she was surprised at how we looked as she had built up a picture in her mind from thinking about us next door grieving so much and then when she saw us we didn't look like her picture. She had thought I would be blonde like her and smaller and Rennie would be dark and a little bigger from the sound of his voice.

We talked about people's looks for a while and how they so often didn't seem to fit a person until you got used to them, and how people didn't seem to fit their names, either, half the time. "My name's Opal Decker and don't you think of a brunette with a name like that? And somebody kind of big?"

"Opal," I said, sort of tasting it—it was a new sound, a name I'd never thought of before.

"Ope for short," Rennie said, and she nodded.

"I never hear Opal, just Ope. I heard you kids calling each other Rennie and Gay, so I guess it's Gail but I can't figure that Rennie."

"Reynal."

"What?"

"Reynal," Rennie repeated. "Like my Dad."

"For Pete's sake," Ope said, "And I thought Opal took the cake."

Aunt Sue came in then and explained that there was some French on her side of the family which accounted for names like Reynal and Suzanne.

"It isn't Gail," I told Ope. "It's Gloria. I wish I'd been named Renee or Nicole but my mother's hobby was seeing old movies and she admired Gloria Swanson." Her own name was Elizabeth, I added, which I thought had dignity but was too long. Ope nodded in agreement. "My father said Gloria was too long, too," I told her. "So he started calling me Gay when I was a baby, and it stuck."

I realized then that we were talking about my parents, not as if they were alive, but fondly and almost as though we could remember them now and not worry about feeling quite so much pain.

Then Aunt Sue said that she had the big room across the hall from her own free and cleaned up now and we could move into it as soon as she had another bed put in. She said that she would have a carpenter come and build a divider so we could each have a room out of it, or almost. (When she finally got a carpenter to come over, though, Rennie didn't want the partition as he wanted to be able to *see* me if he woke up in the night.)

"I want to get you a radio of your own, too," Aunt Sue added, "but right now I want to try to get hold of that carpenter again." She shook her head. "It's hard sometimes getting help for small jobs.''

When she had gone, Ope said that she had lived around here all her life and didn't know any carpenters, could we imagine? When there must be dozens of them in this part of town alone. She explained, though, that this was because she had grown up on a farm outside of town. Then she asked about where we had come from and Rennie and I told her about Mom and Dad and the house we'd had in Blyington where Dad had been a teller in the bank and about school and our friends. Ope saw Rennie's face screwing up and she said, very fast, ''Well, Penn City is a lot bigger so the school will be, too, and with more kids you're both bound to make new friends fast and besides there's more to do here. We've got a zoo and an amusement park which I'd like to take you to on my first day off which would be Saturday if you're ready, or else a day next week that I'd try to get off from the dress shop, or maybe next week end.'' Rennie said this Saturday would be fine if the zoo had elephants or hippopotomases, as size was what impressed him in animals.

Ope said if that was the way it was, why, she'd take us to a museum where they had dinosaurs. Rennie, who had begun to like her, now gave her that look he uses for grown-ups who tell whoppers. He didn't mind fibbing as such, being pretty good at it himself, but coming from anybody over about sixteen (Ope was twenty) it was like talking down, and that always made him mad. But Ope said, ''Not real ones, of course. I took it for granted you'd know that. I'm sorry.'' Rennie looked uncertain and she said, ''Well, I forgot for a minute you're new here—I just had the crazy feeling there for a second I'd known you two characters longer than I have. Anyway, these dinos are made up to look like they did a long time ago—what's the word they use?''

''Replicas?'' I asked.

''Yeah. Say, that's not bad for your age, to know that word.''

"Well, we had it last year in school," I said modestly, "and I just happened to remember."

"She just happened to feel like showing off," Rennie said, the first time he had said anything like that or smiled since the accident.

"I probably had it in school, too," Ope said, "but it's something to remember it—I mean I'm not too good with words, okay, but nothing special. I'm good at clothes, though. I can sew and even design and I can fix up an ordinary pattern so people take notice—not because it's loud or anything," she assured, looking at me. "I mean in good taste with everything fitting in right, the lines and materials and all."

I nodded, impressed, because things like that tended to mix me up. My only distinction was that I would be the youngest one in eighth grade here, because in Blyington way back a few of us had been allowed to skip second grade.

"How many dinosaurs are there?" Rennie asked.

"I don't know, I haven't been in that part—I just heard about it—but probably quite a few. How about Saturday for the zoo and Sunday for the museum, then?"

"Great," Rennie said, and I saw Ope smile a little. I remember thinking that it was a better smile, sweeter somehow, than if it had been a great big one.

When she left, the room smelled spicy just the way she did. When I'm old enough to use perfume, I thought, I'll find out what this is. It was like a mixture of cinnamon and woodsmoke and although that sounds kind of awful put like that, it smelled just wonderful to me then, and very lady-like, too. But uncritical as I was at twelve and especially of Ope, I knew that she used too much of it. I supposed that she saved her subtlety for her designs and color combinations.

Aunt Sue told me later that Ope worked downtown at Marianne's Dress Shoppe and really did have a way with cloth and a needle. "Wouldn't it be easier to use the vac?" I asked. "I mean, it's faster than sweeping, isn't it?" Aunt Sue was sweeping the upstairs hall, and I saw that the vacuum cleaner stood silent beside her.

"Yes, but it doesn't reach quite all the places a broom does. I sweep the dust kitties and such from the edges and corners to the center and then the vac picks them right up." She smiled and raised the broom to the ceiling. "And try getting the cobwebs up here with the vac."

"Well, how about me running the vac for you? You must have to do a lot of cleaning in this big house."

"Oh, not so much. The guests take care of their own rooms, and I don't mind the halls and bathrooms. It's the only exercise I get."

"I'd like to help, though."

"Oh." She was silent for a moment. "Of course you would. Well, when school starts the nicest thing you and Rennie could do is make me proud of you, your conduct and your grades, but till then—let's see, the one job around here I've never cared much for is the yard work. If you mean it, you go ahead outside and see what you'd like to tackle there."

So I took care of the yard, which wasn't very large, mowing and weeding in the summer and raking in the fall. Rennie helped that first day and never afterward, and he spent most of that first day standing on top of a big, half-embedded rock at the edge of the yard, pretending that he was king of the hill. "You think this Ope really means it?" he asked, "About taking us to the museum? And the zoo?" He scowled. "Some people talk and that's *all* they do."

"Sure she means it."

"Well, I sure hope so."

She meant it. On Saturday we took a bus to the zoo and on Sunday we saw the dinosaurs, but we didn't go on the bus. We rode in the car of a rather sullen young man named Paul Punty who, Ope whispered to me by the brontosaurus skeleton, had had a date with her to go to a movie. "But I forgot all about that until this morning and then I called him and told him that I'd thought of something a lot more exciting to do."

"I don't think he thinks dinosaurs are very exciting," I said.

"Don't mind him," Ope said airily. "He can act more bored than anybody I ever knew in my life. Anyway," she added, "I don't think I'll be seeing him any more after today."

"Why not?" I started to say, thought better of it, and then asked anyway.

"Oh, you know, he sort of pouts when he doesn't get his own way, and all he wants to do is go to movies and then go park somewhere, and besides that he's jealous."

"I guess he likes you," I said, and I remember wondering what kind of young man was going to like me some day—a jealous, pouty, good-looking one like Paul Punty? "I guess he likes you a lot."

"Not so much he won't forget me in a week."

The way you will him? I wondered, or will you—he's so handsome with a kind of noble looking face. "Do you forget things easy?" I asked.

"Not important things," she answered. "Huh uh, don't you worry about that. I never forget anything that matters."

Rennie didn't even notice that Paul was less than entranced by the dinosaurs—he was too engrossed by everything to bother about anybody else's reaction. He thanked both Ope and Paul profusely at the end of the day. "I sure like dinos," he said. "They're the closest thing to dragons."

"Gee," Ope said, smiling and yet thoughtfully, "we'll have to do this again, then, maybe next week, okay?"

"Okay," Rennie said. Paul said nothing. I don't

remember ever seeing him again. Ope and Rennie and I made the next trip by bus and the next one in a blue sports roadster, compliments of Fred Blake, not as good looking as Paul—rather homely, in fact, but a lot friendlier. He took us to the museum and on picnics and for rides in the country, and he always started out with one arm around Ope until after a block or two, she made him use both hands to drive. Once we went to a rodeo and Rennie ate too much ice cream and caramel corn so that Fred had to take him into the men's room where he could be sick with a little privacy.

"I should've watched that closer," Ope said, looking sad. "That's me, Ope the dope."

"No, you're not," I said, "you're no dope. You—you're wonderful!" And I started to cry, which probably embarrassed her—I know it did me—but she didn't say anything, and I stopped before Fred and Rennie came back. I thought how neither Rennie nor I had cried after that first week, and I knew that all the things Ope thought up for us to do had a lot to do with it. We were too busy to think about things we couldn't do anything about and start to feel sorry for ourselves.

When school began we found out that Ope had been right—we made new friends right away, though Rennie had more than I did. I wanted to spend as much time as I could with Ope—she always had interesting ideas about things to do and never acted as if I was too young for her to be bothered with. Aunt Sue said she was more of a kid than I was, actually, and if it wasn't for her flair for sewing and the fact that she went out with young men, why, Opal would seem more like a twelve-year-old than I did.

Sometimes Ope asked Fred to drive us to her parents' farm, about ten miles away, for Sunday dinner and the afternoon. She had a large family ("my people" she called them) and they all looked like her, the same face repeating itself over and over on different size bodies. I wondered what it would be like to belong to a family of fourteen, not even counting cousins and uncles and so forth, as Aunt Sue and Rennie and I were the only ones left of either the Thatchers or the Elliotts. There would always be plenty of company in an army like that, of course, and somebody to help if you needed it, but the Decker kids fought and snarled quite a bit, too, and lived packed together, and I decided that I liked my own, more independent position better. They were wonderful people, though, simple and generous and a little coarse, and comfortable to be with.

Halloween came and Ope said, "You and Rennie and me—we're going out and soap some windows." And we did. We also helped to put out a fire that somebody had started on an elderly couple's front porch and stayed to have cocoa and doughnuts with them. Then we rang some doorbells and collected apples and candy and handfuls of popcorn, drew funny faces in soap on all the first floor windows of a warehouse by the railroad tracks and went home where I practiced my cheerleader's chants for the coming football game between our junior high and our biggest rival.

The cheers fascinated Ope. "I wish we'd had cheerleading when I was in school," she said. "Honest to Pete, in the country like that, they just never gave it a thought, and I bet it would've been fun. 'Oskee-wa-wa,'" she howled along with me as we squatted in the living room, making sweeping motions with our hands. "'Oskee-wee-wee!"

"Oom-ba-ba," we said, rising and holding our arms above our heads, "oom-bee-bee! Fight, team, FIGHT!"

"Stars!" Aunt Sue said mildly and Rennie, grinning, said, "They're both dingalings."

The next week was Rennie's birthday and Ope pointed out that anybody was only ten once and said we ought to give him a surprise party, with a gang of his friends, since it was still warm enough to be outside for a couple of hours at a time if you kept moving. We could have a weinie roast, she said, with a bonfire and maybe some cowboy and Indian and army type games with plenty of yelling and running around.

"Don't worry," I told her, "with Rennie there is always plenty of that."

"I know," she said, "so we'll just get some weinies and buns, a great big cake—we can bake two or three just to be on the safe side—and a couple gallons of ice cream. That ought to about do it, except for a real nice present. What does he want, Gay?"

"What doesn't he want, you mean."

"Well, okay, if there's nothing special, then let's just go through the stores and see what we can see."

This was why we were in Mooth's variety store the next day, Ope at one toy counter and I at another. Between us, we finally selected an assortment of guns, two of them with holsters and the rifle with its own long sheath, rolls of caps, and a model car that looked quite a lot like Fred's, all of which Ope paid for since I had no money. Aunt Sue gave Rennie and me allowances, but I hadn't saved any of mine. "Don't worry," Ope said when I mentioned paying her back later, "you're going to pay right now. We're going to buy some paper and ribbons and you're going to wrap up every one of these odd size presents that they never give you boxes for in this place. That'll more than pay your share, believe you me."

"Okay." I giggled then, a sound I made often when Ope was with me. When I have daughters and they giggle, I won't object—it means they've got something to giggle about, it means they feel good about life—it's fun and exciting. "I think I'll wrap up a bottle of water, too, for his squirt gun and see how long it takes him to figure out what it's for. Maybe I'll put a goofy label on it." Like fire water, I thought.

"Think up a doozy, then," Ope advised. "He's a pretty sharp little cookie, that Rennie."

"Yup," I said, secretly proud of him, "it shouldn't take him more than a couple of hours to figure out he's supposed to put water in a squirt gun."

At the ribbon counter, Ope said, "How about you picking out the paper and stuff and then a card and I'll meet you back here in a few minutes. I want to see if I can get my mom a new nightie."

"Okay." After I had put the paper and ribbons in a pile on the counter I went to the card rack, looking at the happy birthday, brother and happy birthday, pal cards. I finally decided on one that said happy birthday, nephew because it had a big picture of a gun on it and I thought that Aunt Sue would like the nephew part. Rennie didn't pay much attention to cards, anyway, any more than he did wrappings. He ripped the paper any old way to get at the presents and that's why I had chosen plain blue paper and let the fancy part be the ribbons. I could save those and use them again later, for other packages or hair ribbons or—

I glanced up then, at Ope two counters over. She had gone from the lingerie counter over to the scarves and handkerchiefs and as I looked at her and smiled toward her, thinking how little and blonde and pretty she was besides being such a good egg and so much fun, she reached out for a pink lacy handkerchief. I thought she would feel it and hold it up for a better look and then put it down to inspect another, but with a quick motion she balled the kerchief in her hand and whisked it into her coat pocket.

I gaped at her, stunned. I could feel the smile disappear from my face as my mouth opened in shock. I had seen it but I couldn't believe it. I couldn't believe it, but I had seen it. Ope had swiped the handkerchief— stolen it—and she had done it quickly and efficiently, as if she'd had practice.

At first I couldn't seem to move my head, it felt so rigid, but I managed to swivel my eyes. As far as I could tell, nobody else had noticed what Ope had done. Everybody seemed to be going about his business just as if the world had not swayed and threatened to fall over on top of me.

Ope turned and I looked away, my neck still stiff but at least able to turn, my knees weak but still able to support me. I reached blindly for a card on the rack and held it out as she came toward me. "All ready to go, sweetie?" she asked, her voice light and high—not exactly merry or pleased but kind of excited. I wondered if she had stolen things before and I wondered if she would again.

If she did do it again, would somebody see her? This worried me, and I decided that from now on I had better stay close to her and let her know that I was watching her, not so that she would feel bad or suspect that I knew what she had done but so that she wouldn't feel alone and free to take something that didn't belong to her.

I wondered what she could possibly want with the handkerchief, anyway. It was a cheap, frilly little thing and she could have bought it easily for a small fraction of what she had paid for Rennie's gifts. It could not have been worth any more than the card, in fact. And Ope was not one to worry about money or to be ungenerous with it. I was completely puzzled, but I couldn't bring myself to ask her about it. If I mentioned it, she would be embarrassed and ashamed. I knew that I would be if somebody knew that I had stolen something.

If my mother had known about the ring I'd taken from a dime store about a year ago, how would I have felt? As if I wanted to die, that's how. And I was a child, not a grownup like Ope, even if I was just as tall. Somebody twenty years old had no business being a thief. Well, actually, no age had that right but if a child just did it once, then you could more or less forget it, I thought. I hadn't really wanted the ring, either, but I still couldn't understand Ope's stealing that handkerchief. It was beyond me, and I was silent all the way home. Ope didn't seem to notice—she chattered more than usual, enough for both of us.

I decided not to tell anybody, not even Aunt Sue, although I badly wanted to ask her for some sort of explanation. I brooded about it all the next day, couldn't concentrate in school, and skipped cheerleader practice. Then on Saturday, when Rennie's party was in full swing with Ope tearing around having as much fun as any of the boys, Aunt Sue tweaked my ear and said, "What's ailing you lately? You don't pay attention, you don't eat, and you got Rennie a birthday card that said 'Happy birthday, Grandma.'"

I wanted to tell her, but I kept quiet, afraid that if I talked about it at all, even once, then I might not be careful enough from then on and might give Ope's secret away without meaning to.

The next hours were like the worst nightmare anybody could imagine. We heard Ope scream and rushed over to her. She was kneeling beside Rennie who was stretched out on the ground with his eyes closed and his head bleeding. Aunt Sue ran into the house and called an ambulance while Ope and I and all those small boys waited and worried about how badly Rennie was hurt and how long he would be unconscious.

He never woke up. He had stumbled over the rake, which I had left out, and fallen, hitting his head on the big rock near the edge of the yard. It was one of those very unfortunate accidents where everything goes wrong— first, stumbling near the rock and then falling at just the angle to make it a fatal blow.

A real freak, the ambulance intern said. Rennie died that night.

Later on, I cried for days, until I was exhausted, but

that night I sat in the hospital waiting room, dry-eyed and too stunned to speak, hardly aware of what was going on around me, not hearing the words when a nurse spoke to me and knowing she was speaking only by seeing the movements of her lips. I saw the worried expression on her face without responding to it. Everything seemed unreal.

Finally, Aunt Sue sent me home with Ope. She was going to call a taxi but a policeman who had brought someone to the hospital and who was ready to leave offered us a ride. On the way, Ope tried to comfort me. "I know how you feel," she said. "I really do. One of my brothers died two years ago—he drowned in the creek—and I remember how I felt."

Nothing will ever be the same now, I thought. Nothing could ever be right again.

Ope's soft voice sounded in my ears. I wished she would be quiet. I didn't want to hear anyone say anything.

Why hadn't I put the rake away? Why had I left it out on the ground?

"—but, honey," Ope was saying, "you do get back to normal. I know."

My mouth opened and words blurted out. "If you're so normal, how come you steal things from stores?" The secret I had held so tightly inside me flew out into the air and then everything was quiet again. Nobody spoke.

Then I began to feel anguish about Rennie. Pain started to seep in through the shock.

It was weeks later, after I had cried myself sick night after night while Ope and Aunt Sue watched helplessly and after Aunt Sue had taken me on that long bus trip to Yellowstone Park, that I realized how I had betrayed Ope. When we came back from Wyoming, I learned that she had been caught shoplifting and had been taken or sent away, no one seemed to know exactly where.

I was convinced that the policeman who had driven us home from the hospital had been the one to arrest her, and I felt sad and guilty for a long time.

It was almost three years before I saw Ope again. One Sunday afternoon near Christmas the doorbell rang and there she was, standing on the porch, the same as ever with her bright hair and eyes and smile. She hugged me and beckoned to a young man in a car at the curb and then hugged me again.

She still used too much of that same spicy perfume and it still seemed wonderful to me. "Oh, Ope, I thought you'd forgotten me."

"Why, that's crazy." She stepped back and looked at me. "I told you I never forget what's important." Her smile flashed again. "Now hang on to your hat, hon—I'm married! This is Kermie."

Kermit Downer was somebody you'd never notice in a crowd until he looked at Ope and his face lit up and made them both special.

"You're going to spend a couple of days with us," Ope said. "We live in Springfield now."

"Really? Springfield? That's not so far from Blyington." I hadn't seen my hometown for over three years.

"Throw some p.j.'s and a toothbrush in a bag while I talk to your Aunt Sue," Ope said, and soon we were on our way.

We went through Blyington's outskirts and Kermit offered to drive into town so I could see my old neighborhood, but I said I could go there the next day. It would be only about an hour's bus ride. I wanted to be my myself when I went back to the scene I had loved and been torn away from. Also, I was eager to talk to Ope alone and thought that while I was helping her get dinner ready I could catch up on some history that she might not want Kermit to hear.

Their apartment was small and old, but Ope had made it cozy and colorful and I'm glad I thought to say so because both of them looked so pleased and proud.

Kermit got out the checker board and I sort of hate to play checkers, but I could see that Ope wanted me to keep him company instead of gossiping with her in the kitchen. So I jumped red men with my blacks and ended up losing four games in a row, while Kermit tried not to grin, and it wasn't till after dinner when he was looking at some western on TV that I had a chance to talk to Ope.

She washed and I dried and for a while we kept up the reminiscing and questioning and answering we'd started in the car, and then Ope said, "I've thought about Rennie a lot. He was a good little kid."

I could think about Rennie by then without choking up, of course, but I still felt sad every time I was reminded of him and so I didn't say anything.

After a minute, Ope said, "I guess you wondered what happened to me when you got back from your trip."

I nodded. "I sent you a card from Yellowstone."

"I got it, hon." She paused. "I guess I should've sent you a letter or something, but I'm terrible about writing. I mean, every time I pick up a pencil my brain goes numb. Anyway, they didn't want me to get in touch with anybody for a while."

I picked up another plate and polished it. "Who's they?"

"Oh, the doctors at this hospital I went to. After I got arrested, see, I went to Philadelphia and got a job there and went to this place—clinic, they call it—three times a week. That was what the judge here said I had to do or else go to jail, so —" Ope shrugged. "I talked to three or four doctors there at first and then later on just the one. He asked me all kinds of questions and all about when I was a kid and what my people were like and so on." She rinsed the silverware and put it in a pan that was still kind of slimy with detergent, so I took it out and rinsed it again and rinsed the pan. Ope didn't seem to notice. She was staring out the window into the back yard, but it was already dark and she couldn't have seen anything but her own reflection.

"It took a long time." Ope was looking down at the sink now. "But he finally said I was cured."

I was curious, but she was vague about details. "The doc said now I had *insight* but the way I figure it, I just sort of grew out of it, you know?"

I shook my head but she wasn't looking at me. "Anyway, I don't swipe things any more. I don't even want to."

"Good," I said, relieved.

"But I still don't know why I did in the first place." Then her face brightened. "A while after I quit the clinic I met Kermie. Oh —" she glanced over at me— "he knows all about that swiping business, so don't worry about saying anything."

"Okay." I knew she wasn't referring to the time I *had* mentioned it, in the police car. Ope doesn't operate that way. If she has something to say, she says it right out.

"We went together for about six months and then got married and Kermie heard about this job in the factory here, so we moved."

"I'm glad it worked out okay for you, Ope. I was worried about you. Especially—I mean, I'm the one who—" I'd wanted a chance for years to talk to her about this, and now I couldn't even finish the sentence.

"Oh, shoot, Gay, I never blamed you for that. I knew you weren't yourself that night. I thought you knew that." She frowned into the dish water for a moment and then looked back to me. "Gee, if I'd known you felt like that, I *would've* written you, no fooling."

"Well, I was afraid that policeman was the one who caught you, and that would make it my fault."

"He wasn't the one, but I heard that he'd tipped off the cop who *did* catch me. Anyway, to tell you the truth, it was a relief when they arrested me. Maybe it sounds crazy to you, but that's the way I felt."

"Like now somebody would help you?"

"That's it. That's what the judge said, too, that they'd try to help me."

Kermit called out then that he was getting lonesome, so we went in the living room and watched TV until after the late news and then Ope made up a bed for me on the couch.

Next morning after eggs and toast and two cups of cocoa, I took the bus to Blyington. I explored my old haunts and learned that everything really did seem smaller than I remembered, just as I'd always heard. Otherwise, though, the neighborhood and the people, too, seemed just about the same.

I looked up some of my former friends and discovered that we were all very glad to see each other but that after a few old memories had been exchanged, we didn't really have much to talk about. We were going to different schools now and were interested in different things, and in a way this was a little sad but in another way it was the best thing that could have happened. It was sort of like giving something a decent burial so that real forgetting could begin.

I walked past the house where Mother and Dad and Rennie and I had lived. I remembered where every stick of furniture had been in each room and the color of the walls and how the kitchen door warped and stuck in rainy weather. I thought about going up the walk and knocking and asking if I could look inside the house, but I knew that I didn't really want to go in, so I cut across the back yard, past the big elm tree where we'd had our tire swing, and went on across town to the bus station and back to Ope's without stopping or feeling sorry about anything.

When Ope and Kermit drove me back to Aunt Sue's, we stopped off at the Decker farm and I saw Ope's "people" again. They welcomed me as if we were old friends and since then, after I got my license and could borrow a car, I'd driven out there sometimes to say hello. It made me feel good somehow just to be with such down-to-earth, simple people who knew and liked me. Also, I could keep up with news of Ope that way. She and Kermit had moved from Springfield after only three months, going first to Ohio and then to Maryland.

Now, nearly two years had gone by since my visit, and this time they were living in Penn City. I looked forward to seeing Ope, and I wondered what she and Sandy would think of each other.

6

I saw Ope the very next day. Sandy and I were just pulling away from the curb in front of my house when Ope came around the corner and walked down the block toward us. Explaining to Sandy that she was an old friend, I braked and waited until she came near enough to hail.

Her eyes widened as she saw me behind the wheel of the Jaguar, and narrowed again with her smile as I introduced Sandy. "Hi!" Her earrings swung as she stepped back and looked again at the car. "I've always wondered if these Jags rode as smooth as they look."

I wanted to tell her to hop in and find out, but I hesitated, not knowing how Sandy would feel about this. He turned to me and smiled. "Gay wouldn't mind showing you."

It wasn't the first time I had wanted to kiss him, but I really had to fight off my impulse now—he was so handsome and sweet. My feelings must have shown on my face, as I heard Ope stifle a giggle before she asked, "Room for me in front?"

Sandy opened the door and slid over toward me to make room for Ope when she gestured for him not to get out. It was the closest I'd been to him—his arm pressed against my shoulder, and I had a little trouble with the gears for a second or so.

"Listen," Ope said a couple of blocks later, after she

had marveled at her luck in catching me at home when a minute later she would have missed both us and the fun of the ride, "you want to do me a big favor, hon?"

"Sure."

"Can we go out to my people's?" I glanced over at her and saw her unscrew her earrings and rub her ears, an old habit of hers. "I mean if it wouldn't take you out of your way." She paused for a second. "If you two have other plans, though, just let it go."

There was a tenseness about her voice that made me look at her again, but her profile told me nothing. "No trouble, Ope, We'll swing over that way."

"Oh, good." Her tone relaxed. "They've been expecting me for over a week now and I haven't made it out there yet. Kermie needs the car to get to work and I—you remember Kermit, don't you, Gay?"

"Sure. How is he?"

"Great. Just great. He's been working overtime a lot at the plant, though, and what with getting settled and all, we haven't had a chance to go anywhere and I know my people've been wondering why I haven't showed up. My mom never figures a phone call's worth anything," she added for Sandy's benefit, "when I'm only ten miles away."

I glanced at Sandy to see if her chatter bothered him but he was smiling a little and so I relaxed, too. His arm touching my shoulder was warm, making me feel affectionate toward the whole world.

The Deckers swarmed toward us like bees as we drove into the yard, and they opened the doors and began to pull us out even before the car came to a stop so that I had to yank at the hand brake and try to defend myself in the same second. That family will kill you with kindness.

After I got my bearings I looked around for Sandy. He was surrounded—besieged is a better word—by Pearl and Ruby and Topaz (the boys have ordinary names but the girls are all jewels) and he looked rather bewildered.

I tried to fight my way toward him and had plowed through a half dozen little Deckers only to be stopped by Mrs. Decker's very ample bosom. She had all but smothered Ope in a bear hug and now it was my turn. When she let loose, I saw that Tom and Bill, two of the older boys, were standing protectively beside Sandy and shooing the jewels away, so I thought that he would be all right and allowed myself to be swept toward the house by Mrs. Decker. Emerald and Jade, the three-year-old twins (called the double Deckers) who always dressed up to their names, tagged along looking like tiny green peas.

Mrs. Decker had some of her terrific bean soup simmering on the kitchen range. It is really a stew with chunks of pork and whole tomatoes and onions, plus any leftovers, thrown into it. It takes a lot of stirring so it won't burn on the bottom, and I more or less automatically picked up the big wooden spoon and stirred until Diamond and Sapphire wandered into the kitchen and took over.

Mrs. Decker and Ope had been standing on the back porch for a while, embracing and exclaiming as they always did, but now Mrs. Decker bustled inside and started mixing bread dough and Ope, I noticed through the window (which had millions of little, jammy fingerprints smeared on it), was headed across the yard toward Sandy who was still with Tom and Bill and the jewels.

"Pearl and Ruby and Topaz can't get enough lookin' at your boyfriend," Mrs. Decker remarked, pointing a floury thumb toward the group. "Opal's goin' to show him around a little."

"Good," I said, wondering just how interesting Sandy could find a barn, a corncrib, and some assorted animals.

"Guess you know what we're havin' for dinner," she said comfortably. The noon meal was dinner and the evening meal was supper. "Hope he likes beans and they like him."

Then something happened that I'll always be ashamed of. No matter how long I live, I'll cringe whenever I think of the next few minutes.

Until she mentioned dinner, I hadn't thought of Sandy's eating there, but now I did. Sandy would be expected to wash from the bowl in the kitchen sink and dry his hands with the same towel the others used. The food would be served in thick bowls and would seem plain and starchy to him. Everything would be coarse and hearty. Everybody would reach in front of everybody else for those thick slabs of bread and chew noisily, and I would seem to be one of them.

Dad Decker and Dick would come in from the fields in their dirty bib overalls and sweaty workshirts, and Dad Decker would make sly jokes directed toward my "new boyfriend" while the others laughed. All in fun, yes, and the kind of companionship I'd enjoyed with this friendly family for years, but nothing I wanted Sandy to see.

"He's a good lookin' boy," Mrs. Decker said. "Dresses nice, too, and my—that car!" She chuckled. "You did yourself proud there, Gay."

I saw Sandy and Ope come out of the barn and walk toward the corncrib. Mrs. Decker shouted at Diamond. "Stir it up good, now! We don't want no burned-up beans today!"

"I—I guess we won't stay, Mrs. Decker. I mean, we've got a lunch packed and we have to get back and—"

She moved back as a reflected ray of sun stabbed her eyes, and her broad face looked paler for a moment. "Oh." Her smile had faded. "That's too bad. Well —" She added water to her flour mixture.

"I mean, it's just that—"

My voice trailed off and she said, "Why, sure, Gay, don't you worry your head a bit about it." She smiled over at me and I turned back to the window. "So you'll stay next time."

I couldn't seem to let it go at that. I felt that I hadn't been tactful enough, that I had hurt her. "Mrs. Decker," I began, "I didn't mean—"

She waited and when I didn't, couldn't, go on, she reached across the table and patted my arm. "Now, Gay, don't you think I can see things? Naturally, your young man wouldn't think much of this old dirty farm." She nodded toward Sandy who was standing by the corncrib now, talking to Jackie, the youngest boy. "You know which side your bread's buttered on," she finished calmly. "I wouldn't let nothing stand in my way, either, if I was you."

Her tone was kind, but I felt that the words were like some kind of epitaph. I could see them written on my tombstone: Here lies Gay Elliott. She got what she wanted because she never let nothing stand in her way.

I wanted to cry nice big soothing, self-pitying tears. No matter what words either of us used, we both understood that I was ashamed of her and her family and her home.

Mrs. Decker turned back to her bread and I rushed out of the house, stumbled on the top step of the porch, regained my balance just in time to keep from breaking my neck in a fall to the bottom, and started toward Sandy.

When I was half way to the crib, Ope called out, "Guess we'd better be getting back, you think, Gay?"

"Guess so." I was glad that my voice was fairly steady.

Ope came toward me, with Pearl, Ruby, and Topaz following her. "I mean, you've got somewhere to go, don't you?"

I knew that she wanted to stay with her people. "Listen, Ope, you want us to come back for you, maybe about six?"

"Nah, it's out of your way. Besides, I've got to get Kermie's supper going before that. Just give me a sec to tell Mom goodbye."

She ran to the house and the jewels and I joined Sandy and Jackie. Jackie's eyes were shining as he held up a stick of wood. "See this, Gay? Sandy made me a whistle." He looked up at Sandy and smiled until his eyes were slits. Then he blew the whistle with such *zest* that the rest of us held our ears. His cheeks hollowed out and his eyes glittered. He blew and blew and smiled and smiled. Sandy put his jackknife back in his pocket and laughed, and Jackie stopped blowing and laughed, too.

Ope came back into the yard, raised both arms to wave, and yelled, "So long, sprouts. See you next time."

Immediately, her brothers and sisters crowded around her. "Aw, Ope, you goin'?" "Hey, Ope, when you comin' back?"

When we finally managed to get into the car and out of the yard onto the road, Jackie ran after us, shouting, "Hey, Sandy, if you stayed till dark you could help me ketch fireflies!"

Ope shouted back and waved, but Sandy's laugh had that same hollow ring I'd noticed before when he was tired, and I was glad that we were leaving.

After we had dropped Ope off at her apartment, we headed toward our glen. I was still depressed, but Sandy, who was always so quiet and slow himself, didn't seem to notice my silence. I was grateful again that he never seemed to need small talk because I don't think I could have chattered just then if my life had depended on it.

I knew that I could go back to the farm some other time. Mrs. Decker would welcome me and act the same as always, but I didn't think that she would ever really quite trust me again. How could she?

I saw then that I had liked the idea of having "simple" friends because it made me seem smarter and nicer.

Yet I really did love them.

And why hadn't I given Sandy a chance to show that he could appreciate the Deckers as they were?

But our relationship, Sandy's and mine, was so young and tender, and I would have died if anything had hurt it. I wasn't ready to test it—there wasn't room for other people in it.

I thought of telling him about Ope. I felt that he would understand about her kleptomania and all and that in some way this would lift my spirits. I wasn't sure why—it was only a feeling. Then I decided not to say anything. It would be like throwing Ope into a wastebasket, and I had been enough of a monster for one day.

Later on, when Sandy and I knew each other better, I would tell him all about how I felt today, and he would understand.

I was still depressed when we got to the woods, but for some reason, sitting there on the blanket beside Sandy in our own little hideaway, I suddenly wanted to talk. It might have been partly because Sandy said we should eat the dessert right away before it melted—food always picks me up—and this was special. Something wonderful had been added to vanilla ice cream, and I asked what it was.

Creme de cacao, Sandy told me. He had poked a spoon handle into the center of the mound and poured liqueur into the hole. It had all melted and blended just enough. I was really enchanted and I remember thinking quite ruefully that up till then my idea of an ice cream treat had been a hot butterscotch sundae.

I didn't feel hungry after that and let the rest of our picnic stay in the hamper while I talked. I suppose I was trying to run away from my own thoughts by quoting other people's, and I guess I was trying to impress Sandy, too, when at one point I mentioned La Rochefoucauld. "He said things like 'We all have enough strength to bear the misfortune of others' and 'It is not enough that you win—your best friend must also fail.' Well, every time I read something he wrote, I marvel at his perception, but did he have to write *everything*? I mean, it's *always* La Rochefoucauld who said it.''

Anyone but Sandy would have said, ''Oh, Gay, not *always*—you always exaggerate so.''

Then I would have said, ''And you always generalize. You just proved it by saying I always exaggerate.''

And so on and so forth, very futilely. But Sandy only nodded, and I felt that he understood me.

I never once mentioned Ope or her people, didn't even ask him what he'd thought of them. I simply babbled on about how I felt about various things, and he listened closely as he always did. ''Books, for example,'' I remember saying, ''I don't have anything against certain ones *just* because we had to read them in school. There's *John Brown's Body* which I loved and didn't expect to like at all from hearing the title. Every line in it is beautiful. 'Oh, to lie by her side in the darkness.' How could it be said any better?''

Then I tensed up, wondering what had made me quote that particular line and if Sandy would react to it, but his expression stayed the same, and so I relaxed.

''And I don't have anything against liking what people my age are supposed to be fascinated by. I mean, I don't feel I have to be different and not like Thomas Wolfe, for example, just because we hear that sixteen-year-olds so often ''discover'' him. I love his wild rhythm— 'O lost, and by the wind grieved ghost, come back again.' I wish he was still alive so I could talk to him. I'd like to tell him that life isn't really all that bad and I'd like to ask him if it really is all that wonderful.''

Sandy looked a little bit puzzled, but I couldn't think of good examples to make my point, so I went on. ''And I don't have a prejudice against a writer and his ideas because they were big a long time ago but considered sort of dated now. Freud, for instance—I don't know how well his methods *work*, but it certainly is interesting to read about them.''

"Books?" Sandy said, rather abruptly, so that I stopped talking and waited to see why he had spoken so suddenly. Then, after quite a long pause, he added, "I don't think books should be censored."

"I don't, either," I said, wondering just what that had to do with what I'd been saying. "Practically everything else is and I'd hate to see books go under. Did you have any special ones in mind?"

He shook his head and I tried to think of some books which should not have been censored and couldn't think of any, so I said, "There are some books I'd hate to think of missing, though. I mean, they weren't censored or anything but I'm glad I didn't miss reading them. There's *The Outward Room* by Millen Brand and there's *Ramona*. And the *Book of Songs*—you know, Chinese poetry. And poetry and music together, like Schubert's *Serenade*. It has such sweetness."

I knew that Sandy would understand what I meant. "When I think about missing any of those," I added, "why, it almost breaks my heart."

"Poetry?" He seemed to be thinking about it, and after another long pause he said, "Do you like poetry? Then I'll give you this book."

He took a book from the back seat of the car and brought it to me. I opened at random to a page and saw a poem by William Blake. I'd read *Tiger, Tiger* and *The Little Black Boy*, but this one was new to me. I read it aloud:

> "Piping down the valleys wild,
> Piping songs of pleasant glee,
> On a cloud I saw a child,
> And he laughing said to me:
> "'Pipe a song about a Lamb!'
> So I piped with merry cheer.
> 'Piper, pipe that song again;'
> So I piped: he wept to hear."

I looked up then and Sandy was smiling at me. "Oh, thanks," I said, and hugged the little book up close to me, knowing that I was going to love it.

Sandy was a perfect person. My depression lifted as I thought of his wanting to please me, and doing it, and smiling. And suddenly I felt hungry again, ready for our lunch, which I knew would be perfect, too.

7

Velma had just promised to try to get the name of a doctor for me when Mr. James came over to our table. "Can't you see me going to dear old Dr. Horseley for something like *this*?" I'd said. "First he'd faint and then he'd call Aunt Sue."

"Like I said, I'll ask around."

"Ask around about what?" Mr. James grinned when Velma and I jumped. With all the lunch time noise around us and with my problem on our minds, neither of us had noticed him approaching. "Say, Gay," he went on before we had a chance to make up an answer, "I've got a compliment for you. Mrs. Carlyle stopped in here for dinner the other night, and we mentioned you. She told me what a nice girl you are."

"Oh." I hardly knew what to say. "I didn't know you knew Mrs. Carlyle." Somehow I couldn't quite imagine her in the Rathole.

"Well, I didn't, but she introduced herself. We've got a mutual friend or two."

I'll bet she had to stretch for that, I thought uncharitably, and then felt ashamed. Mr. James is not exactly high society but he's straight with us, never talks down or gets too touchy, and he's always been especially all right with me, calling me first whenever his kids needed a sitter and recommending me to others.

"Charming is what she called you. I told her you were one of the best kids around, that I'd trust you with anything."

I fidgeted a little because Velma was giving me one of her Mona Lisa smirks. "Well, thanks, Mr. James."

"Sure, kid. Any time." He started to go and then turned back. "Say, she's pretty darned charming herself."

"Yes, she certainly is."

When he had gone, Velma pushed her empty plate away and smiled. "Sounds to me like Mama's checking up on you."

"Looks like I passed, too." I always feel that I should have a flip answer for Velma.

"You hope, doll. Actually, I bet she thinks nobody's good enough for sonny."

"Maybe nobody is." In my opinion, nobody was. I couldn't blame Mrs. Carlyle for her concern. And I knew that she was concerned. I'd seen quite a lot of her in the past month and I thought she was simply great. To begin with, she had meant it about asking Aunt Sue and me for lunch and, later on, had dropped in at our house and had coffee. (I was at work that morning and when I learned that she had come, my first thought was that I hoped she hadn't seen my room. I'd been in a hurry and hadn't made the bed, but Aunt Sue, who I suspect can read minds, at least mine, said that she had given her a tour of the house but had made my bed first.)

I could smile now at my picture of Mrs. Carlyle before I met her—a dowager looking through her lorgnette. I had even imagined her saying—in a balloon like the ones used in comic strips—"You peasant! You are not good enough to shine my son's boots!"

How ridiculous it seemed now that I knew her and saw how kind and gracious she was.

I was more and more impressed with her. For

example, one night Sandy and I went to a marvelous place for dinner. The service was so smooth and automatic that I knew everything had been prearranged, and I thought that Sandy had done it. But when the cake came, he explained that his mother had taken care of all the details. We were celebrating her birthday, but she hadn't come along because she thought that we'd have more fun this way. She wanted to be the gift-giver and, knowing her, I knew that she meant it without any strings, and it *was* fun. Sandy and I took turns blowing out the candles, and we danced until the waiters began stacking the chairs and practically threw us out. I don't know when I've enjoyed a birthday so much.

With a mother like that, I couldn't help feeling that Sandy was even more than I had thought, although his being any better hadn't seemed possible. I envied him this lovely, kind, wise mother and even though I'd told myself over and over not to sigh about things I couldn't have, such as marriage to Sandy, I thought about what a wonderful mother-in-law she would be.

For one thing, I could talk to her. We had exchanged confidences, with me telling her about my tentative plans to go to college and my doubts about the value of it. She had said that of course I could do it if that's what I really wanted, and then added, quite simply, "College isn't necessary for everyone." I felt that I knew where Sandy got his quality of understanding.

She understood him, too, and one day after he had played one of his own piano compositions for us and then gone to his room, she had talked to me about him. I stood in front of the painting I liked best, not knowing whether the tears in my eyes were because of the colors and shapes of Sandy's painting or his playing, and listened to her tell me about his moodiness and his need for rest, telling me with an air of frankness that made me feel we were friends. "You'll find him abrupt sometimes, dear," she said, "and preoccupied and, as now, too exhausted for amenities." Her little laugh seemed self-conscious and I realized that it wasn't easy for her to be saying this. "I suppose you could call it artistic temperament."

"Well, if anyone has a right to it," I said, "Sandy has."

"Oh, Gay." Her fingers brushed my sleeve and I turned to see those large, dark eyes of hers practically melt. "You always say the right thing."

I knew that I was one of the last people on earth to deserve that particular compliment, but I was somehow still glad that she'd given it to me.

"I do appreciate your interest in him." Those soft, dark eyes were concerned, and I understood that she wanted to know how I felt about him but that she wouldn't ask. I would have done almost anything in the world for her, but I couldn't answer her question. My thoughts were so frantic: If she thinks I'm falling in love with him, she might try to stop us from seeing each other....I know I'm not good enough for him, but I can't help my feelings and it's too late now to try to be sensible...

So I stood there and didn't answer. I couldn't tell her these thoughts any more than I could tell her that I planned to seduce him.

Sandy must have told her about the Rathole. I'd taken him there one night, to show him off—I admit it. We sat at this same table. Sandy had sat where Velma was now and everybody in the place had looked at us, either openly staring or sneaking glances from time to time. I knew they were impressed with Sandy, and I had never been so proud in my entire life. It wasn't just that he was new and handsome and well dressed, but he had a way of concentrating on me, of listening intently to me, as if I was the only person in the world who counted, and I knew that everybody else could see this, too.

Then Velma had come over to be introduced and that

started a trend so that a dozen more friends joined us, pushing tables together and ordering cokes and making quite a lot of noise. I was glad that Harold wasn't there as everybody would have watched his reaction and he'd have been both hurt and mad and trying not to show it. Velma said, "I see why you dumped Harold, but I don't see how you can keep this one." She wasn't being mean, just honest, and she kept her voice down so that nobody else heard.

A while later, though, when somebody asked a question, Velma poked me and whispered, "Did you notice Mr. Barton over there? No, over by the juke box. He keeps staring at your boy. Hey, maybe it takes one to know one."

"That isn't funny, Velma."

"Who's trying to be? On second thought, though, maybe not. Sandy's too thin and pretty. The real fairies are mostly muscle men these days, nice and butch."

"Oh, Vel, cut it out." But after that I couldn't help noticing that while Mr. Barton *was* looking at Sandy with interest, Sandy paid absolutely no attention to him.

We left soon because I could see that all the chatter of six people talking to him at once was wearing Sandy out. He was trying, but his laugh was strained and hollow, and I knew that he was tired.

Sandy. I'd sat mooning long enough. I picked up my purse and dug out enough change for the sandwich I'd eaten, and a tip.

"Hey, what's your hurry?" Velma asked. "We've got twenty minutes yet."

"I'm meeting Sandy in ten," I said. "Listen, Vel, can you tell Miss O'Connor that I've got cramps or something?"

"I guess so." She frowned at me. "For the third time this week." When I said nothing, she added, "This might be the last straw."

"So be it." Truthfully, I had expected the sack last week. I was on the job every morning, as Sandy composed then, but less than half the afternoons. When Sandy wanted to be with me, I didn't let work stand in our way.

Velma shrugged and then brightened as she looked up. "There's Harold."

I stood as he came toward us, and curtsied, offering him my chair. He had called me several times since our evening at The Hanging Eye, but I'd always said I was busy. Finally he'd more or less given up and told me to call him when I had some free time.

Ope had called me several times, too, I reminded myself then, and talked to Aunt Sue since I was hardly ever at home these days. But one of these days soon I'd call Ope. I wanted to see her and have a good long talk with her.

Harold stood by our table, blinking at me. "What's your rush, Gay?"

"She's too good for the likes of us," Velma said, "First it was college and now she's decided she'd do better with a rich, handsome guy."

Harold didn't say anything, just stood there looking awkward and kind of sad. I managed to smile at Velma, although I wanted to slap her, and walked away, calling back over my shoulder, "So long, you two. Have an exciting twenty minutes." I really needed her help quite desperately.

8

The woman sitting next to me in the doctor's office used a cologne that reminded me a little of Sandy's shaving lotion, and I sat there missing him and feeling miserable. I was glad that Velma had taken a morning off to come with me, as I didn't think I could have waited alone.

She sat there pretty glum and quiet for her, turning Tokie's picture post card around and around in her hands and never really seeing the bear standing beside Old Faithful. So finally I reached over and took back the card before its edges got too frayed. Tokie's message was: SAVE THIS PITCHER FOR ME. I MEAN PLEAS.

"Dr. Harvey Button," Velma had told me and I'd said, "You've got to be kidding." Part of the reason I like Velma in spite of all the things I don't like about her is that she will go out of her way to help (like finding out about a doctor) without acting shocked or superior. Or cheerful. Thank goodness, she seemed just as nervous as I was.

The woman with the lotion smell stood up when the nurse called her name, and I watched her walk into the inner office and wondered what would be there for me when my turn came.

"My sister mentioned that a friend of hers was using the pill," Velma had said, "and so I just sort of casually asked what her doctor's name was. I had to lead up to it and I thought Sis would get suspicious, but she just laughed because she thought the name was funny."

"Ordinarily, I would, too, I guess."

"Well, anyway, that's the best I could do, so make an appointment."

"Okay. And thanks, Vel." And so here we were, leafing through old dogeared magazines while the horse-faced nurse tapped the temples of her glasses against her teeth and frowned at us.

I was too restless and tense to concentrate on anything, and I ached all over. Even my teeth ached. It was Sandy. I couldn't think of anybody but him.

I used to wish I had a lot of sex appeal, but I didn't care about that anymore as long as I had what *he* wanted. If I did. And if I didn't appeal to him, then what difference did it make who else liked me?

I wished I didn't talk about Sandy so much. I knew I was driving poor sweet Aunt Sue out of her mind, but I couldn't seem to help mentioning something about him every other minute. I just couldn't let up—I *had* to say his name because then, somehow, he seemed closer to me.

Last year I had crushes on three different boys, but now I knew that those feelings had been nothing.

Sandy had all the things I admire most: brains, talent, understanding, kindness, sensitivity. And he was so handsome. Usually there are things wrong with people's looks even when they are very attractive, but I couldn't see even one tiny flaw in Sandy's face. I hurt inside thinking of his face.

I know that it isn't possible to find perfection in any one person, but I thought that I had found it in Sandy. It just seemed as if he was the only one who could answer all the questions I'd been asking myself. And whenever I wasn't with him, I'd think that I couldn't stand it a minute longer without him. I wanted to run to him and throw my arms around him and hold him tight.

Once, in our woods, I had a terrible urge to hug him. I wanted to grab him and it was all I could do to restrain myself. He was bent forward, mixing colors on his palette (I loved to sit for hours and watch him paint) and when he glanced up at me, I saw him from this new perspective and it was like seeing him for the first time all over again, only more clearly. His good looks struck at me, they really did, almost like a blow or a dash of cold water in my face, and I felt very weak for several seconds.

Then he smiled and I thought I was going to pass out. Things seemed to blur—the outline of his head was fuzzy and the sky was gray—and I could feel my head wobbling. He sat up straight then and he looked alarmed. "Gay, are you all right?"

"S-sure," I managed finally. "I'm okay, Sandy." And as he turned back to his paints, I was grateful that I could feel like that even though it had been a little frightening. I knew that he would be embarrassed if he'd known why I'd seemed strange for a moment.

"I'll bet you've kissed a lot of girls," I said and then felt myself blushing awfully. It was such a coy and immature and horrible thing to say. I wished I could die on the spot.

I sat there, chewing my lip, wanting to bite off my tongue, but Sandy smiled and cupped my face in his hands. His smile was sad and sweet.

I closed my eyes when he kissed me. I didn't feel terrible any longer. I felt wonderful.

He was sweet in so many ways. For instance, when he found out that I liked milk he began to bring it along with our lunches. I remember drinking it that first time and then trying to wipe off the mustache it left before Sandy noticed, but he took my hand away from my mouth and said to leave the milk there. It was touching, he said, and something seemed to gallop inside me when he said it.

And once he took my hand and studied it and said,

"You have nice hands, Gay."

"They're too big." They really are rather large and I'd hoped he wouldn't notice them.

"No. They're well shaped and strong, competent." He squeezed my hand then and let it go. "I like them."

"Thank you, Sandy." He never said anything he didn't mean, and it was very good to know that a part of me pleased him enough to comment on it.

"You're lovely," he said, softly and without looking at me, and I couldn't finish my lunch. It was the strangest feeling and I had trouble trying to put it into a thought, but it was as if I'd lost my appetite because I'd been fed with something I needed more than food.

One time I commented on his understanding of people and he shook his head soberly. "I'm really a schizoid character," he said, "interested in my own little world."

I grinned at him. "Oh, Sandy."

"True. And I'm hard to get along with, too."

I remember thinking that we are all willing to mention our big faults, but how many of us will admit to something unglamorous like grumpiness?

"You'll see," Sandy said.

I smiled and nodded toward his cup of wine. "In vino veritas?" I asked, and immediately was seized by a horrible thought: did I pronounce that right? I read a lot and have a fairly large vocabulary from that, but I have never heard some of the words spoken and also I took French in school, not Latin, and I thought how embarrassing it would be if I'd said it wrong. I'd seem pretentious and phony to Sandy.

But it must have been okay as he smiled back (without hesitating even a tiny bit as he might have if he'd been being tactful) and said—very cleverly, I thought— "Sure, un veritable realite de loup."

I was glad that he wasn't always telling jokes, the way so many boys did to keep the conversation going. I was tired of that and besides, memorized jokes cover up things and keep you from getting to know people.

He was quiet and he often answered my questions with only a "Yes" or a "No" but I listened to changes in his voice and looked at the way he moved his hands and felt that I knew what he was thinking.

It was sweet to be with Sandy, and also very exciting. We were together now almost every evening (Aunt Sue said, "My stars, why is he rushing you so?", but since we never stayed out late, she didn't object.) and it was wonderful. We went to restaurants where I learned what food could be and should be, and I remember thinking, with horror, that if not for Sandy I might have gone all my life not knowing this. We went to concerts and plays and I began to see what else I'd been missing. There was this entire, fascinating city I hadn't known about before and as we explored it, Sandy made me feel that it was actually laid out at our feet and that there was nothing in it that we couldn't have.

I learned how to drive everywhere in town. At first I was a little nervous about the traffic. Sandy hated it and suggested taxis, but when I said it was fun to drive the Jag and feel that I controlled its power, he smiled and shrugged and handed me the keys. I hadn't driven Fritz's old Dodge for weeks, and what a relief not to have to ask that old troll for a favor!

We were treated like royalty wherever we went. Every waiter in the city seemed to know Sandy and every one of them fell over himself to give us the best service possible. We had our own sets of china and silver, for instance, at each restaurant, and to be honest, I loved drinking coffee from the same cup I'd used the last visit and knowing that no one else had touched it in the meantime. It made me feel special, as absolutely everything about being with Sandy always did.

Of course, all of this cost Sandy a fortune. The bills

were large and his tips were really far too generous, often as much as the check itself, but this was how Sandy obviously wanted to spend his money and there was always plenty of it, so I never objected.

He'd bought himself a whole retinue, but I could tell that it wasn't only the huge tips. Everyone appreciated his good manners and, to judge from their questions about his painting and music, they all respected his talent, too.

Only one thing ever dampened an evening, and even that only puzzled me. I couldn't understand that girl's attitude, subtle as it was. I've forgotten her last name, but Sandy called her Carla and I got the impression that he used to date her. She stopped at our table only long enough to say hello to Sandy and ask about Mrs. Carlyle's health and a few things like that as some people were waiting for her, but this was long enough to see that she was quite sophisticated. I mean she was beautiful and witty and used to the best and sort of amused by everything. She was just the type I'd always thought Sandy would be interested in, and I wouldn't have blamed her if she'd given me an unfriendly glance.

I could never hope to look like her or have her style, but why should she look at me with pity? It was quite puzzling. Actually, *I* felt sorry for *her* and for all the other people in the world who weren't with Sandy.

But I forgot her in the pleasure of the delicious food and exciting atmosphere and great service.

Everyone wanted to please us. When we prowled through the Chinatown food stores and curio shops, Sandy was greeted by name and deferred to and, although I knew that the Carlyles were good customers who kept their charge accounts busy, I still felt that these clerks regarded Sandy as a friend as well as a client.

It was even a treat to go to the amusement park, where I'd been many times before, because Sandy knew the workers and performers and it was interesting to talk to them backstage. I especially remember the shy midget who kept brushing his hat and puffing on his oversized cigar and the roustabout with the scarred face who mentioned that Mrs. Carlyle had dropped by the other day with flowers for his wife, who'd had a touch of bronchitis. "Wish we could do something for you folks for a change," he said and Sandy smiled and said, "Well, maybe you can some day." I thought, why couldn't I have acted as well as Sandy, that day at Decker's farm?

Sandy seemed perfect to me. Not only was I happy with him, but I was learning, too, and improving myself. For example, I'd learned quite a lot from watching Sandy paint. I'd never be good at it myself, but I was more conscious now of shapes and colors around me, and I enjoyed them more. I'd hate to have missed this awareness.

And Sandy had encouraged me to practice more on the guitar and to make up verses and melodies for it. "You have a flair for folk songs," he'd said, "and a pretty good voice and ear." Then he'd praised my very modest efforts at composing so that I wanted to keep trying. I wanted to write a song as good and as different as the ones he played—even though I knew I couldn't.

Also, listening to Sandy speak made me want to improve my own way of talking. My speech used to be rather faddy and slangy, but now I try to be more original.

I'd changed through that part of the summer in other ways, too. For instance, I wouldn't've picked up a hitchhiker. Somehow I thought more of the possible consequences *before* I acted.

Sandy was good for me and it was good to be alive and to be with him.

Of course I was still immature. I wanted to run away with him and I had childish daydreams of saving him from death or injury—pulling him back in the nick of time when a speeding car was bearing down on him or rushing into a burning house and dragging him out, alive but unconscious from smoke. And I wrote over and over again: Gay Carlyle. Gloria Elliott Carlyle. Mrs. Alexander Sanford Carlyle III. Sandy. I love you. Sandy. Sandy.

I knew that he didn't love me, but I had hopes that he would before long. His loving me was my idea of heaven, because I felt that my search was over, that I'd found what I'd been looking for.

There was only one other thing missing in our relationship. Sandy had kissed me that once, and that was all. I found this very frustrating and I'd given the problem a lot of thought. I knew that Sandy was sensitive and rather shy and that I would have to take the initiative. I wanted his arms around me and I knew that if he ever held me I wouldn't be able to draw any lines. I'd want to go on and on.

But I wanted to consider him as he had me, and this meant not forcing an obligation on him—in other words, no pregnancy. I needed the pill which was why I was sitting so tensely in Dr. Harvey Button's waiting room.

We had been there only twenty minutes, but I thought my turn would never come. Part of a verse of *Black is the Color* kept running through my head:

> "....But still I hope the time will come
> When you and I shall be as one."

Sandy fascinated me. I thought of him all the time. If I couldn't have him, I thought I would go out of my mind.

At last the woman with the nice cologne came out of the inner office, and the long-nosed nurse motioned for me to go in.

I sat there paralyzed.

"Doctor will see you now," Horsey said, but I couldn't seem to move.

Then Velma asked, "You want me to go in with you?"

"Oh, gosh, *yes!*"

I clutched at her arm and when she smiled and walked into the little room with me I was terribly grateful. I felt close to her, as if we were sisters, and I automatically forgave her for everything she'd ever done that I hadn't liked.

Dr. Button rose as we entered and since I was so nervous this made me want to giggle. Actually, his gesture told me that he was probably a little old-fashioned, as if his idea of protecting "young womanhood" might be to *not* give them contraceptives.

Maybe he would even think I was dirty for wanting them. I gulped and sat down in the chair he indicated. Velma sat in the other chair by his desk, her legs crossed, and altogether looking pretty cool. I wished that I had her poise.

"Well, young ladies, what can I do for you?" I saw a tiny bald spot on the top of his head as he bent over the sheet of paper in his hand. "Which one is the patient?" He glanced up at Velma. "Miss Elliott?"

"No," Velma said, nodding toward me. "She's the patient and she wants the pill."

I felt like gasping, even though I'm used to Velma's directness, but Dr. Button merely looked puzzled. "The pill?"

"Birth control pills," Velma explained. "You know, so she won't get pregnant."

"Oh." He tapped his fingers on the desk top. "Of course. Well, I'm afraid I—"

"You've given them out to others," Velma said. "I know that."

Dr. Button frowned and then decided to ignore her. "It's *Miss* Elliott, isn't it?" he asked me. "And you're sixteen?"

I'd written eighteen on the paper, but now I nodded and felt trapped.

"Well, it's true that I have prescribed the pill, as you call it, but not for young unmarried girls. I'm sorry."

His brown eyes were warm and kind and I felt that he really was sorry. His jaw was set firmly, though, and I knew that there would be no budging him. I got up to go and Velma said, "Now, wait a minute."

"It's no use, Vel."

She gave Dr. Button an exasperated look. "Why don't you let her tell you why she wants it?"

"I know why. She's in love." He had all the answers which is always so annoying in middle-aged people, but at least he didn't sigh or lecture or probe or say anything about telling our parents.

"Come on, Velma, let's go." At that point, I simply wanted out.

"I thought you doctors were supposed to help people," Velma said, "not preach."

"I'm *not* preaching," he said, quite offended.

"It wouldn't be much help if she got pregnant, would it?" Velma asked.

Dr. Button had risen when I did, but now he sat down again. "No, it wouldn't," he answered and I could see his Adam's apple bob when he swallowed. "But I've thought about this problem before—more than you seem to think, Miss — ah, young lady. And I've decided not to help unmarried teen-agers to get contraceptives. I may be wrong—" He stopped, apparently expecting Velma to agree, but she only stared at him. "Well," he finished, "I just may be wrong, but there it is."

"Okay, okay," Velma said mildly. "Thanks for your time, doc."

I fumbled in my purse, but Dr. Button said, "No charge," and lit a cigarette.

"Thanks." Mostly, I felt tired, although I really had expected better luck than this.

Velma was standing at the door by then, with her hand

on the knob, and she kept her voice casual. "Guess you'll just have to use the rhythm system, Gay."

"Oh, Lord." Dr. Button choked on a mouthful of smoke. "Don't do that."

"She won't if she can scratch up the pill somewhere," Velma said, but he just shook his head, and so we left.

Velma grinned all the way down the hall and stairs and when we were outside she said, "He wasn't so bad for an old creep, was he?"

But I didn't smile. My mind was too busy making plans, as I had no intention of giving up because of this one disappointment. My jaw was set just as firmly as Dr. Harvey Button's, and I knew that Sandy was for me and that our belonging to each other was only a matter of time.

This is what I *told* myself, but what I *did* was all of a sudden start to cry. Velma said "Hey!" I guess she was really surprised, especially when I went on and on. I was quiet about it, but I couldn't seem to stop the tears from running down my face. She took my arm and walked me over to a bench at a bus stop and sat there making soothing noises until the tears stopped, and then we went to a very neat little Italian restaurant and had lunch.

Velma devoured a huge plate of lasagna but I just looked at the minestrone I'd ordered. It smelled very good, but I wasn't hungry. Then after the waiter went to get her spumoni, Velma said, "Listen, Gay, not only are there other doctors in the world—there're other methods, too."

I'd known that all along, of course, but somehow her saying it seemed to cheer me up, at least enough to eat half the bowl of soup.

9

The inevitable happened. I took off from work one too many afternoons and Miss O'Connor fired me. I had seen more of Sandy than I had of the office, and so now someone else was sitting at my desk, typing and copying rows of numbers and filing reports.

I didn't miss the work, which was dull, and I wouldn't have wanted to lose even one hour of precious time with Sandy, but I did miss the pay checks, and I felt that I had let Aunt Sue down. She hadn't said a word, but I knew that I should be paying in something to help her out. Mrs. Unger's room had been vacant all summer, and we were just making expenses.

I looked for another job, but everyone wanted full time help. I did insist upon doing the hall cleaning in the mornings, but that wasn't like contributing cash. I was ashamed to be selfish enough to put my own pleasures first, but I couldn't see less of Sandy—I simply couldn't. I counted the hours and the minutes from one meeting to the next and resented the time not spent with him.

Also, he was changing. It wasn't anything I could put my finger on, but he seemed to need me more. It was something I *felt*. Outwardly, while seeing me more often than ever, he paid less attention to me than he ever had.

His silent periods were longer and more frequent. He was moody and sad and sometimes irritable. When I mentioned this to Mrs. Carlyle, she gave my ear lobe a little tug and said, "Try to bear with him, dear. He's planning a new painting, and I know so well how difficult he can be when his creative juices are stirring."

She always, *always*, made me feel better. She was so reasonable, so practical and articulate. Why hadn't I thought of Sandy's art? I resolved to try to see more clearly into the motives of others. It would do me good and surely would make Sandy think better of me.

"You're good for him, dear," Mrs. Carlyle told me one day. "I'm so grateful that he's chosen someone like you."

I didn't ask what she meant by "someone like me." My head whirled at the thought that she believed he had *chosen* me. *Me!*

Surely she wouldn't have said what she did if she thought of me only as a convenient companion for Sandy's summer. She was too sincere for that, too honest. And summer was nearly over. Now was the time for her to be hinting at that, letting me down easy, before Sandy went back to school.

She could have said things like, "Thank you, Gay, for helping to make his vacation so pleasant" or (with a little laugh) "Don't expect Sandy to write often, Gay. Heavens, I'm lucky if I hear once a month that he's still alive, and even then it's usually a collect phone call to tell me that he's overdrawn again."

I'd braced myself for remarks like that. I knew that she was interested in knowing how I felt about Sandy (she wouldn't want me hurt any more than was necessary if I was falling in love with him) but didn't want to pry. So partly to spare her feelings, too, and partly because I didn't want to do or say anything that might keep me from Sandy, I answered lightly so that his mother and I could relax and remain friends.

She seemed to accept this and I thought that she might

even appreciate my tact until one day she remarked a bit wryly that it was possible to understand why I was called Gay.

I wanted to tell her that I loved Sandy and that I wanted her approval. But I knew that I wasn't in his league, that he wasn't in love with me, and I couldn't bring myself to confess that I was wild about her son and planning to seduce him.

She was fond of me, but I knew this would be going too far, so I kept my conversation light and "Gay" and hoped for a miracle to happen before summer ended and Sandy would say goodbye.

I never fooled her, though, not for a minute.

She understood, too, more than I realized then, how much Sandy needed me. For example, even though she had not seen Sandy drive his car up the curb and half onto the sidewalk when he came for me one day, she never questioned my doing *all* of the driving from then on, even to my keeping the Jag parked in front of my house and calling for Sandy every afternoon. She even thanked me once for taking such good care of him. "You're a sweet, considerate person, Gay," she said and I blushed, knowing myself to be the opposite but unwilling to give up the credit I didn't deserve.

I wanted her praise and I justified my silence by remembering that Sandy did need me.

He was terribly absent-minded, for one thing, even forgetting to eat half the time, and he daydreamed more than ever and was more and more wrapped up in himself and his painting. When I talked to him, he'd get this faraway look in his eyes, and he'd shrug and never say very much. Or he'd begin to speak and then trail off so that what he'd said didn't make sense.

I accepted this and tried not to bother him when he was working, but one thing did hurt—although I tried not to show it. One morning I went to a beauty shop downtown and had my hair streaked—the combination of blonde and light brown really looked nice, I thought, and I was no longer drab. I also bought new make-up and spent quite a lot of time learning how to use it for maximum effect. Mrs. Carlyle had been marvelously generous with grooming tips and advice about clothes. She never volunteered information, afraid to hurt my feelings, but was always there as solid as a rock whenever I asked for her opinion, and I felt that I had learned quite a bit from her.

So there I was, all dressed up and made up and everything, and Sandy didn't even notice! Mrs. Carlyle told me how nice I looked (as Aunt Sue had, and the roomers who saw me) but the opinion that counted was Sandy's.

Later on, he did compliment me, but I was sure that his mother had reminded him to notice and comment. I told myself that I couldn't expect to compete with oil paints and inspired composition, and that I would have to love Sandy as he was—that is, more or less incomplete as far as other people were concerned. And I respected his difference, his absorption in creativity so that everyday details were bypassed.

Sometimes I got on his nerves. He said I talked too loud and too much, and often when I was driving he would duck and say "Look out!" when the other car was yards away, or he would tense up without saying anything, as if he thought I wouldn't bring us back alive. I couldn't understand how he could *see* paintings and *hear* music the way he did and yet not be able to park a car straight or drive in his own lane or how he could yell at me for shouting when I was speaking in an ordinary tone.

I urged him to get his eyes and ears checked, but he snapped at me and I dropped the subject, wondering if he could be a little vain about wearing glasses or a hearing aid. Actually, I thought Sandy would look good in anything, even one of those old-fashioned trumpet type hearing aids.

And yet he was quite tolerant about my own attempts at painting. He praised the colors I used, even though I could see that they were raw and wild compared with the lovely, subtle ones in his own paintings. I did notice that his own style seemed to be changing—it was bolder and less disciplined now—and I wondered if I could possibly be influencing him for the worse.

In spite of his encouragement, I knew that I could never be really good, but in a way I was glad of this. I wasn't so sure that I wanted genius like Sandy's if his tension and frustration with his work had to be part of the package. I was only mediocre, but I was a lot happier than he was.

He liked to have me with him. He said I calmed him by just being there and by being myself, and this made me feel that I had some purpose on this earth. One day we were sitting quietly in our piece of the woods—for a change I was the one daydreaming—when suddenly Sandy tossed aside his brush and said, "I really like you, Gay."

I could hardly stand it, I felt so wonderful. I was honestly more pleased than if he had said "I love you." Because that was something I was willing to wait for, but I couldn't have taken it if he hadn't *liked* me right then. It was the best thing to build on. I mean, I knew there would be a time when I couldn't bear it if he didn't love me, but I would come to that later. The fact that he liked me now and told me so was a very sweet thing.

Then he asked, "Don't you want to know why?"

"Oh, yes, Sandy, why?"

He smiled and touched my little finger with his little finger and said, "Because you never try to cut off my balls."

I must have looked quite startled, as he laughed and

kissed my finger and then turned to the hamper and poured us some sparkling grape juice.

We dropped the subject, but I kept wondering why he had said that. Surely he didn't mean Mrs. Carlyle had her thumb on his neck? She seemed so non-possessive. She would say things like "Sandy is happiest with a quiet routine," but this was true. Music in the mornings, painting in the afternoons, entertainment in the evenings. He had done well on this schedule. His mother was so understanding that his remark seemed unfair to her.

I couldn't always soothe him. I mentioned The Hanging Eye to him (he frowned at the name, although he'd been amused by the Rathole) and told him about the colored lights flashing as the combo played. "It's supposed to get you sort of high without drugs," I said, and added, "It's a phony place."

Sandy shrugged. "Everything's phony." Then he said, "It's a good feeling—I like it. No need for machines, though." He snapped on his transistor radio. "I can see the lights. Red, green, yellow. Dancing in the air." He turned off the radio. "Any sounds. Your voice."

I thought he was joking and said so, but he shook his head. "You made some pretty green balls just then—with specks of yellow."

"Oh, Sandy."

"That was orange. Try for blue."

"You're making fun of me!"

"Too much green. Try again."

"Oh, San—"

"There it is! Blue discs, dozens of them! Good girl!"

I shouldn't have laughed. I knew that he was serious. I wish I hadn't laughed at the wrong time. I sounded so crude and unfeeling. I could never seem to express myself the way I wanted to. No matter how I tried, what I wanted to express didn't come out and what I wanted left inside came pouring out. It embarrassed me and scared me.

Still, Sandy wouldn't have been so annoyed with me at the beginning of the summer. He was touchier now.

And he didn't always soothe me, either. Once when we were browsing through a department store, I thought I had lost Sandy. I hurried to catch up, stumbling, and then I saw the top of his head above the crowd in front of me. "Sandy!" But he didn't hear me.

I hated to shout again, but I did, and when there was no answer, I ran around the edge of the crowd, almost falling down the stairs, and finally came close to him. "Sandy!" I was panting.

"Oh, Gay, there you are." He took my arm. "Have you finished looking around?"

We started down the aisle. I glanced up at him and saw a small, malevolent smile turning up one corner of his mouth and I understood then that he had heard me and had enjoyed my frantic scrambling toward him. It was only a little lie, but I felt very hurt.

But we had such a store of good memories! Not just the major ones, which were wonderful, but also a whole pile of sweet, funny little ones. Such as the time we were walking down the street behind three little girls about nine years old. Some men sitting in front of a store smiled at them and one said, "I'll take the doll in the middle."

Quick as a hummingbird, the pretty little dark girl in the center darted to the right of one of her friends, making *her* the one in the middle.

"Oh, no, you don't!" The second girl hopped to the third girl's left and *she* screeched and ran around the first one. They kept this up—a new game called Don't Get Caught in the Middle.

Sandy and I laughed for two blocks and then stood watching them as they turned onto a side street. One of them picked up a cap some other child had dropped, and I predicted smugly, "They'll hang it on a fire hydrant so the owner can spot it when he comes back to look for it.

Now if they were *boys*, they'd just kick it a couple of times and go on.''

We saw the little girl drop the hat with great care into a mud puddle, and then each of the three took turns walking over it and grinding it down into the mud before they went merrily on their way. ''What did you say about boys?'' Sandy asked.

Then, on August 17th, I became seventeen. What I wanted most was a kiss from Sandy, and having a birthday made me confident. When I picked him up, he put the hamper and a large gift-wrapped package in the back seat of the Jaguar, and I smiled, thinking that the day was certainly getting off to a good start.

But it turned out to be one of Sandy's more preoccupied days. At first I tried to talk to him, but from his answers I could see that he'd heard only part of what I'd said, and when he hunched his shoulders the way he did when he didn't want to be bothered with my chatter, I decided to give up.

The faraway look was there in his eyes and I knew that he must be thinking about his painting and that talking to him now would only confuse and upset him.

There was a beautiful little cake included in the hamper, but neither of us touched it, and I didn't light the pretty pink candles.

I gathered up the remains of the picnic, returning the napkins and silver to the hamper and putting the food in a paper sack. I don't remember when I first began taking food home with me. I was appalled at the waste (Sandy ate even less now than before—almost nothing) and I couldn't bear to see so much of our lunches left for the squirrels. Also, the rich and different food was such a treat for Aunt Sue, who had always hated to cook ''fancy'', though she's very good at the basics and had made a big point of serving balanced, nutritious meals ever since I had come to live with her.

I was sure that the guitar-shaped package in the back seat was Sandy's birthday present for me, but since he hadn't mentioned it all afternoon, I didn't think I should, either.

I drove him home in silence, both of us depressed. Of course I didn't get kissed, and I felt like 17 going on 70.

In my room a big bouquet of yellow roses was waiting for me. The card said "Love from Sandy," but I wasn't at all surprised when Mrs. Carlyle telephoned a few minutes later to wish me a happy birthday.

"Thank you for the flowers," I told her, "and for the cake, too. It's lovely."

After a brief pause, she asked, "Do you like the guitar, dear? We can exchange it if you'd rather have a different style."

I hardly knew what to say. "Well, I have it here, but—well, I haven't opened the package."

There was another pause before she said, "Did Sandy forget to give it to you? Oh, I'm so sorry, Gay. Please forgive his utter absent-mindedness. As you know, he's planning a new painting and he—" she broke off, and then added, "but I don't have to tell *you*, do I? Do look at the guitar, dear. I'll wait."

I untied the ribbons and sat for a moment touching the polished wood. "It's beautiful, Mrs. Carlyle. Thank you."

She laughed softly. "It's Sandy's doing, Gay. He spent a full morning choosing it last week. I'm so happy that it pleases you."

I did like it—it was a magnificent instrument and much too good for the way I played—but I would have loved it if Sandy had given it to me.

A few days later Sandy gave me the painting, the one both of us liked best, the one I had admired so much the first time I'd seen the Carlyle apartment, the colorful oil painting that wasn't marred by perfection and that made me believe an ideal world was possible.

When he gave it to me, I said, "Oh, Sandy," and when he kissed me, I cried.

My tears seemed to alarm him. He stepped back quickly and I had to clutch his arm to keep him from running from me. I knew that men can react very strangely to a girl's tears, but I was so busy calming Sandy that it wasn't until later that I thought about it and realized that I had really expected *him* to soothe *me*.

We had a nice day together. Sandy was quiet but pleasant and aware of me. I was content to spend the afternoon looking in turn at my gift painting and at Sandy working on preliminary sketches for his new painting.

As soon as I got home, I called to Aunt Sue to look at my surprise. When she didn't answer, I hurried down the hall with the painting and through the empty living room into the kitchen to see Mrs. Anson, an old friend we hadn't seen for months, sitting at the table. Aunt Sue stood by the stove with her hand on the coffee pot handle, but when several seconds went by and she didn't lift the pot or even seem to notice me (although I had *burst* into the room calling her name), I began to realize that something pretty terrible must have happened and given her a shock.

Mrs. Anson spoke then, pointing toward the painting. "That's an odd picture you got there, Gay. All those odd colors splashed together. What's it supposed to be, anyway?" She shook her head and squinted her eyes. "That frame must have cost a fortune."

I was thoroughly confused, wondering how Aunt Sue could stand so rigid and white-faced while Mrs. Anson spoke almost as she always did.

"Dorothy has just come with some bad news," Aunt Sue told me, and Mrs. Anson fidgeted in her chair and looked uncomfortable.

I waited and then went over to Aunt Sue and put my hand on her arm. "It's about Tokie," she said.

"What, Aunt Sue? What about Tokie? Are they back from Yellowstone?" I shook her arm. "Aunt Sue, is Tokie hurt?"

Mrs. Anson sighed. "She's dead," she said, abruptly but not unkindly, just as if she knew that telling me had to be gotten over with.

I felt my hand drop away from Aunt Sue's arm then and saw her move to the table and sit down. I stood by the stove and heard Mrs. Anson say that Tokie had been sitting on a window ledge and had fallen out—all of a sudden—while she was talking to her mother. Ironically, Mrs. Unger had just said, "My God, Tokie, get away from that open window," and Tokie had grinned and said, "Aw, I'm okay, Mom, you worry too much," and then had fallen out—just like that—four stories.

Mrs. Unger ran down all the flights of stairs shrieking like a banshee and swooped up Tokie from the sidewalk and ran, still screaming, down the middle of the street through traffic a mile and a half to a hospital where they had to pry her loose from the body.

The funeral was over and Mrs. Unger had left town, no one knew where. The news didn't filter down in time for us to comfort her or do anything at all but cry by ourselves in the kitchen. Mrs. Anson was embarrassed by our reaction as she hadn't expected to be the bearer of anything but a gossipy tidbit, and she mumbled that if she'd had any idea how much we cared she'd have let us know sooner, at least in time for the funeral. Then she made her excuses and backed away. I don't think she'd ever seen Aunt Sue cry before.

I never heard Tokie play the piano—I doubt that she had time to learn (Mrs. Anson said that Mrs. Unger had moved to that apartment because a music teacher lived on the ground floor of the building), but I wonder if I'll ever hear a piano played again without thinking of her and of Mrs. Unger who had put all her dreams on Tokie's growing up to share a real friendship.

I remembered my parents and Rennie, and I wondered what kind of a world this is where the light goes out for people who were happy and good and for those left who only wanted to love them.

"It wasn't your fault, Aunt Sue," I said. "About Rennie, I mean. I was the one who left the rake on the ground."

"Good heavens, child, I never blamed you." Aunt Sue looked horrified. "I should have checked the yard before the party. And I should have seen to it that none of the boys ran around that rock." She turned her face away. "That rock. I don't know how many times since I've wished I'd had that rock removed before I did."

She'd had it dug up and hauled away the week following Rennie's funeral. "Like locking the barn—" she'd muttered to herself. "But I can't stand the sight of it."

"Nobody's to blame," I said now, wondering why neither of us had thought before that the other might feel guilty and need to talk about it. Some things are better brought out in the open, and some are not. I'd never tell her that I'd had nightmares sometimes for a year afterward, dreaming that she might die and leave me, too.

"I guess I never thanked you for that trip to Yellowstone," I said. "It did help."

Aunt Sue nodded. "When there's something to be done, it's best to do it."

We talked for a while about Rennie and Tokie and my parents, remembering things about them. The first time I watched Tokie while Mrs. Unger went shopping . . . I'd thought Tokie was asleep and had gone to my own room for a book and come back to find Tokie dumping her mother's giant economy size box of face powder down the bathtub drain and singing "Jesus wants me for a sunbeam" . . . Making a fat, sloppy peanut butter and jelly sandwich for Rennie and seeing him grin and hearing

him say, "Gee, thanks, What's-your-name" . . . Coming
home from school and knowing who'd written on the
sidewalk in front of the house "GAY THATCHER
ELLIOTT IS A NUT" . . . The reddish highlights in my
mother's brown hair and my father's long legs that
seemed to tangle when he sat down in his big brown chair
and crossed his knees . . . her soft laugh and his puzzled
smile as he tried to understand her humor . . . Daddy
reading us bedtime stories . . . good, rich chocolatey
desserts which I said weren't really good for us and Dad's
advice: "Well, don't gobble it down so fast, then. Let
the poison in slower" . . . Mother pushing our sleds up
the hill and sliding down with us . . .

And I remembered a couple of spankings I got, once
for cutting off Rennie's curls and once for putting soap in
the bellybuttons of all the gingerbread men Mother had
just baked for us. I must have known that one was coming
because I remembered sitting on the cement step on the
back porch and rubbing my bottom to make it numb.

It didn't hurt any longer to think about those things in
my past, but now I couldn't get Tokie out of my mind. The
day had started so well and ended so badly. I decided to
hang the painting the next day, when life could seem to
begin all over again.

But the next day brought its own problems. When I
dialed Sandy's number to tell him that I was on my way
over, Mrs. Carlyle answered the phone and told me that
Sandy was not there and that she didn't know when he
would return.

I couldn't think of anything to say but "Oh," and for a
moment or two I forgot to listen to Mrs. Carlyle.

".... not so restless since he's been with you this
summer, but his work has put him under a strain lately.
When he can't sleep, sometimes he takes long walks,
alone, and I never know when . . . "

Her voice quivered and when she paused, I asked,

feeling very awkward, "You mean he's, well, run away?"

I didn't hear a click or a dial tone, but there was such a long silence that I thought she might have laid the phone down on the table and walked away. Then she said, "Well, no, Gay, dear," and laughed a little. "He's rather a big boy for that, don't you think?"

I nodded and then realized that she couldn't see a nod, so I said, "Yes, of course, Mrs. Carlyle. I only meant, well, do you mean Sandy's just disappeared?"

"He's taken one of his little trips."

"Has he done this before?" I was confused.

"Sandy likes to get away occasionally, as we all do." Her voice sounded edgy now, and I knew that she was running out of patience with me, so I said, "Well, thank you, Mrs. Carlyle. I'm sorry to have bothered you."

"Why, you haven't bothered me at all, dear." Maybe I'd only imagined that she'd been edgy. After all, Sandy was old enough to take care of himself. "When he comes home, I know he'll get in touch with you."

I thanked her and she said, "Yes, dear. Goodbye."

I wondered where Sandy had gone, and why, but most of all—when would he come back?

I sat by the phone for a whle, missing Sandy, before I called Ope. I hoped that she would come over and cheer me up, and she did.

The first thing she said was, "Hey, you look great! Your hair and everything." Next she asked, "How've you been, anyway? Like your job? You still dating that same guy—Sandy?"

Before I could answer, she added, "You know, he was okay but maybe a little bit of a cold fish, you know?" She clapped her hand over her mouth, and I couldn't help laughing.

"Listen, Gay, maybe I shouldn't've said that. I liked him, honest. You're not mad, are you?"

"Of course not, Ope." I wasn't as for one thing I keep saying that I like people to be frank and so I can't very well get mad when they are. And Ope's telling me what she thought was a sign of friendship. But mostly I just felt sorry for anybody who couldn't fully appreciate Sandy. They were missing so much. And yet, I didn't mention that Sandy had gone off to be by himself.

"He makes me a little nervous, is all," Ope explained. "Nothing I can put my finger on, though—I guess him and me just don't run on the same track." She grinned. "You should hear Pearl and Topaz and the others rave about him—they think he's the handsomest guy alive."

"How's Kermit?" I asked. "And your people?" Ope was not really sold on Sandy. I thought she resented his superiority, since she was used to average men and felt more comfortable with them.

"They're all okay. Mom said to tell you not to be such a stranger."

I relaxed a little. Mrs. Decker hadn't held that day against me.

"Notice anything different about me?" Ope asked, and, automatically, because it was on my mind those days, I looked at her waist and belly. "No such luck, Gay," she said. "We keep trying and hoping, but nothing doing yet."

Obviously, there was no point in asking Ope about the pill. She wouldn't know or care. I looked at her face then, but it seemed the same as always. "I give up."

"I had my ears pierced!" She wore tiny, glittering earrings. "I got so tired of the other kind. I was always losing one of them and they hurt my ears."

"That's great," I said but I was wondering where Ope had *been*. The pierced ear fad had come and gone years before. Then I remembered that Ope was about twenty-five now and so I supposed she'd have to be a little square.

"Say, has your aunt got any of that homemade wine around? Funny, I never liked it but I always miss it. How come, do you think?"

"I guess it's part of the time you used to live here in this house—how you were then and all."

"Yeah, I guess. You're a sharp cookie, Gay." She looked at me thoughtfully. "You know, I always figured you might have brains."

"Oh, I do," I assured her. "I just never use 'em."

"What're you two gigglin' about?" Fritz stuck his big head around the door and then came into the kitchen and sat down at the table with us. "Did I hear somebody say wine?"

"You did if you were listening," Ope said, since she had never been able to stand him, either. "I've changed my mind, though, Gay. I'd rather have coffee."

I poured three cups, as there is an unwritten rule at Aunt Sue's that no one is ever refused coffee but no law that says we have to drink wine with Fritz. He made a point of touching my arm when I brought his cup and I toyed with the idea of spilling coffee on him, but Ope, reading my mind, advised, "The mess wouldn't be worth it," so I only slopped up his saucer.

Fritz put a napkin under his cup and four spoonfuls of sugar in it, took a sip, leaned back in his chair and belched, while Ope and I glanced at each other and away and were careful to keep our expressions blank so we wouldn't explode into a real giggling fit.

Then he told us some quite disgusting story, which he swore was true, since he wouldn't be telling girls *jokes* like that, of course, about a woman he knew who preferred a dog to men. He laughed and wiped his wet gray eyes and waited for our reactions. I was too surprised at the story to say a word, but Ope shrugged and asked if we were supposed to clap and throw money.

Fritz said that, being a gentleman, he wouldn't name the woman but that he saw no harm in describing the dog.

"Oh, I know that dog," Ope said. "He goes down to Sheff's butcher shop every afternoon for a handout." She took a sip of coffee and added blandly, "Well, you've got to admit that he's a mighty handsome dog."

And while Fritz was still staring at her, Ope took my arm and we *swept* out of the room.

"That old bastard," Ope said when we were outside the house. "The crummy old bastard."

"He makes me cringe."

"*I* might throw up." Then Ope began to laugh. "Did you see the look on his face when I said the dog was cute?"

We walked down to Meyers' for a soda, giggling like fools all the way. It was like old times—up to a point.

"Our conversation was filled with "Remember the time —" and "Wasn't it fun —" The time we spent most of a week trying (unsuccessfully) to make up a fairly complicated crossword puzzle and learning that this only *looks* easy. The time we ate tomatoes in Mrs. Hofer's garden until we were ready to burst and then had to lie down flat to hide, with our faces in the mud, when the old dragon came roaring home in her sports car at just the moment we'd decided to leave.

"It seemed like she stuck around forever," Ope said now. "I thought we'd suffocate in all that mud."

"It sure felt good to swim in her pool when she finally left again, though."

"Boy, *didn't* it!"

As Ope and I reminicsed, I thought how once so much of my emotional life had centered around her. I hadn't realized it then, of course, but I could see now how limited she really was, and I knew that even now she would enjoy going back to twelve-year-old games.

Impulsively, I hugged her, and we both nearly fell off our stools. We laughed, but I saw tears in her eyes, and this sobered me in a hurry. "Ope!" I grabbed at her arm, "What's wrong?"

"I've got some bad news."

My heart leaped and fluttered. Not her people, I thought, not one of the Deckers. Oh, God, don't let it be something bad about her people.

"We're packing up again," she said, wincing a little to remind me to stop clutching her arm. "Kerm wants to leave again."

"You practically just got here."

"I know it. It's just been great seeing you again, Gay—and gee, I can't get over how grown-up you are." She broke her straw in two and laid it on the counter beside her glass. "I don't know when I'll see you again. Anyway, I didn't want to mention it the first thing—you know, and throw a wet blanket over our whole day."

I nodded. "Does Kermit have another job, or what?"

"Yeah, about the sixth one so far. The trouble is, Kermie doesn't seem to be ready to settle down in any one town so as soon as we dig into a place and I get to feeling like it's home, why, he starts talking about better job opportunities somewhere else. Then the next thing I know I'm packing to move."

I wanted to say something helpful and couldn't think of a thing.

"The grass is always greener somewhere else for Kerm," Ope said, but fairly cheerfully. Nothing really got her down for long.

"Maybe he'll get tired of moving, too."

"Yeah, that's what Mom says. He'll get it out of his system one of these days."

"I'm sure everything will work out all right," I said, although this is the type of idiotic remark I hate.

"Oh, sure, it'll be okay. I can wait." She grinned then. "Heck, the next place might not be far away and I'll still be close to you and my people, too."

"I'll drink to that." We ordered our third sodas and smiled again, but somehow, to me at least, this goodbye seemed to be the end of something.

And all the while throughout the day (and the next and the next), I kept wondering where Sandy was and when, if ever, I would see him again.

10

Sandy was back home and in one of his moods again. He was sullen when I came to pick him up and wouldn't speak to me. Mrs. Carlyle rode down in the elevator with us and walked with us to the car. Her good-natured small talk and smiling goodbye wave made the day seem a little brighter, and I began to hope that Sandy would cheer up once we got to the woods and could relax.

I supposed that he had a hangover as he had drunk too much the night before. Three scotch and waters wouldn't be too much for most people, I guess, but it seemed to be for Sandy since he'd made such a scene and complained very loudly and unpleasantly about the food. This was one of our favorite restaurants and the food was always delicious, but Sandy insisted that it tasted as if it was coated with ptomaine.

Finally, when our waiter had brought him a completely new dinner, Sandy refused to even taste it and he threw the plate on the floor. I was embarrassed to death and I remember thinking that Sandy was really the most childish, spoiled, self-centered individual I had ever known. The whole world revolved around Alexander Sanford Carlyle the Third.

The waiter helped me get him to the car and then stood back and smiled a little to reassure me. "He'll be all right now, Miss. He always settles down once he gets in the car. He knows he's goin' home."

I was pretty confused at that point and could hear myself stammering. "I—I mean, well, I didn't know he drank. Too much. No, it wasn't too much. But I didn't know it affected him like this. He's been under a strain, but —"

The waiter gave me a strange look. "You been with him all summer, ain't you?"

"Yes, yes, I have, but —"

"Then you got to have a pretty good idea of what's goin' on."

"But I don't. I *don't!*"

"Take it easy. Now, listen, you sure you're okay? You want me to drive?"

"No, I'm okay. I can drive."

I reached for my purse but he smiled again and backed away. "It's already paid for."

I felt quite bitter and cynical on the way back to the Carlyle apartment and thought to myself that we were actually pretty well covered with "Sandy insurance," one of the many things money could buy. He could have acted up at the carnival, for instance, and then the sword swallower or the tattooed man would have helped me with him and said, "It's already been paid for."

Sandy's mood didn't change in the woods. Since he had come home, he'd seemed unhappier and more irritable than ever and the last few days had made me wonder quite often it it was all really worth it and if I wanted to go on with it. Much as I loved Sandy, sometimes I wanted to run away from him.

I'd never been able to make up my mind whether I thought that I ought to keep trying and working for something I wanted or if I thought that if something didn't work out for me fairly soon then it was no good.

But those thoughts were before I met Sandy, and I knew now that he was worth working and waiting for.

He was such a contrast. When he wasn't sad or moody, he was so extremely nice and so in tune with himself.

I didn't want any other complications, though. Sandy was enough, a full time job.

He no longer listened to me attentively. He'd lost interest in what I had to say and had nothing to say himself. I'd always liked his silences because I don't think two people should have to talk all the time, but he was hardly speaking at all lately. I wanted to make contact with him and know him, but so much of the time he seemed to be sunk in his own sad thoughts, and I couldn't get through to him.

He was slower than ever, as if he had to think out each word and each movement. He didn't seem to care about things any more. We sat there in the woods and he told me about his father's death. He had been murdered in a hold-up, and I thought the brief story was gruesome, but Sandy's expression didn't even change. He was really too controlled—I could never be like that. I'd cry when I even thought about it.

I asked him about his plans for returning to school—registration time had come and gone and neither of us had done anything about it—but he only shrugged and wouldn't discuss it.

I tried again. "I always meant to ask you, Sandy—how did you like Ope?"

His face remained blank, and I added, "You know, Opal Decker and that big family on the farm."

He shook his head and I thought good heavens, he doesn't even remember them. It seemed impossible that anyone could forget Ope and all her people, but Sandy had managed.

I couldn't let it alone. "You remember that day we went out to the farm. Well, Mrs. Decker asked me to stay for lunch and —" I was confessing at last and I don't suppose anything could have stopped me. "And I made her feel bad by refusing. I mean, it was like telling her she wasn't good enough."

Sandy said, "You should have killed her," and I had never been so astonished in my life. I wanted to think that he was joking but I'd learned not to laugh until I was sure.

"What—what do you mean?" I asked, but he wouldn't answer. I tried to figure out some reasonable explanation—had he meant that I had as good as killed her, had ruined our friendship by my attitude? Or had he meant that I was right and she was wrong and deserved punishment? I couldn't make sense out of his remark.

"Sandy, what do you mean, I should have killed her?"

He looked at me for a long moment before he said, "I mean you should forget her. Nothing is worth feeling that bad."

"Oh." I had more questions to ask as I wasn't satisfied with this answer, but I'd already irritated him by interrupting his thoughts so I kept quiet.

He sat there with that faraway look in his eyes and seemed to be listening to something I couldn't hear. Everything I'd ever hoped for and dreamed about was part of Sandy and there he sat, staring into space, not even remembering that I was there.

He stared at his palette, studying the little dab of red there as if he'd never seen oil paint before. He rubbed the handle of his brush with his thumb as though the wood was the smoothest, softest, most delightful thing in the world. He didn't look at me at all.

Then he rubbed his hands across his face and rumpled his eyebrows. He began to punch and jab himself with the brush, and I got the weird feeling that he was doing this to make sure that he was really *there*, the way people pinch themselves to make sure things are real and they aren't dreaming.

"Sandy, what's wrong?" I tensed up, expecting his irritation, but he wouldn't speak and that was worse.

He dropped the brush and held his head in his hands. He looked so miserable and I wanted desperately to help and didn't know how. I heard him mutter, "How can I be sure?" and then suddenly I realized that he was crying, very softly, the tears moving in slow, jagged paths down his face. His face was blank, completly expressionless.

I waited, unable to move toward him. His weeping seemed like a private affair, something no one else could comfort.

After a while the tears stopped coming and Sandy dropped his hands to his lap and looked at them for a long time. He studied his hands for several long minutes. Finally, he moved one of his fingers slightly and then was very still again.

He stretched out on the ground and went to sleep. I sat there watching his thin, haggard face and the little tom tom of a pulse pounding in his throat. His shirt and trousers were wrinkled. He'd always been so neat and shining, but lately he didn't seem to care a bit what he wore or how he looked. I felt carefully in his pockets but I couldn't find any sign of liquor or drugs. I wouldn't have known LSD if I'd seen it, but I was looking for it.

Or something, anything, to explain Sandy's behavior.

He had kept his painting hidden from me, kept the back of the canvas toward me all day, and now while he slept I rose and tiptoed to it and looked at it and wished I hadn't. Up until now his paintings had been vivid, but here was this drab, grayish, flat thing looking as if the artist had lost three quarters of his vision and had become color-blind, too. There were four dull gray, distorted people standing against a flat gray background. They had large triangular heads, small leggy bodies and nothing for faces but gray smears.

The painting repelled me and I walked quickly away from it. I took my guitar from the car and then turned back to search under the seats but found nothing.

I sat down and waited until Sandy woke up and then asked if he'd like some lunch. He nodded but didn't eat even one bite, simply ignored the full plate I passed to him. I wasn't hungry, either.

"Gay, I'm sorry I —" His voice trailed off and he frowned. "Why do you always say that?"

"But I didn't say anything."

"I don't know why you always lie."

"Sandy!"

We both sulked for a while and then he said, "I'm sorry I slapped you."

"Slapped me? You didn't." I added, "You'd better not, either, Sandy."

"I'm truly sorry."

He looked sorry and I realized then that he must mean slapped me down verbally, calling me a liar. That had hurt, but he did seem very contrite and so I smiled and said, "That's okay," hoping that we could forget everything strange and unpleasant and start all over.

"We never use the hammock, do we?" he said. "Oh, well, we can use it for a mailbox."

"A mailbox?" I felt a little like an actor on a stage taking my cue. "I wish you would write me a letter, Sandy. I'd like to have a letter from you."

"All right," he said, "but not now." He turned away from me then and I heard that little laugh of his that didn't ring quite true. It sounded as if he was trying to convince himself of something, as if he thought he *should* be laughing but wasn't sure why.

I forced myself to sit there quietly. My own nerves needed calming and I picked up my guitar. I sang some of *To a Faretheewell*, a song we had made up together, Sandy's melody and my words:

". . . *to a faretheewell, right down to a faretheewell* . . ."

I was singing so softly and concentrating on it that I jumped and almost dropped the guitar when Sandy yelled at me. "Shut up! Shut up!" He clapped his hands over his ears. "Don't shout, for God's sake!"

I wondered if he had suddenly gone deaf. Or if I had.

He began to whisper and I leaned forward a little to hear him, but he leaped away from me. He looked both angry and frightened. Had I changed in some way? I felt very confused.

Sandy moaned and his voice was like a sad chant. "I'm forgetting how to see, I'm forgetting how to hear, how to feel, how to —" He broke off and then began again. "I can't remember how to do anything."

I wanted to go to him and put my arms around him and comfort him but I knew that would be a mistake. I thought he wanted understanding but wouldn't understand it, and I sat there apart from him and wished I was dead.

After a minute or two I got up and gathered our things and said, "It's time to go home, Sandy."

"Home?" He looked rather dazed, but he went to the car without protesting.

When we reached his apartment, Sandy went right to his room and I stayed to talk to Mrs. Carlyle. Some kind of odd pride had made me not want to tell anyone, not even Aunt Sue, about Sandy's moods, but today had been more than that and I felt that his mother should know.

So I told her about his behavior and my concern. "I'm worried about him, Mrs. Carlyle," I finished, "and I don't know how to help him."

But she said, "When his new painting is all thought out, I'm sure he'll act civilized again, dear."

When I asked her if that really explained everything, she added, "Unfortunately, he's trying to do too much. The painting would be enough, but there's his composition, too."

"He pulls away from me," I said. "He won't let me near him. I can't share his thoughts or—or—"

She frowned thoughtfully and didn't speak.

"He's so tired and unhappy," I went on, my voice wailing, "and—and so strange. He's like a stranger."

"Well, my dear," she said rather coldly, "you must learn to appreciate the effects of sustained creativity."

I glanced up, startled at her cool tone, and she immediately smiled. "You remind me of a stricken fawn, Gay." She pinched my ear gently. "I didn't mean to wound you, dear."

"I'll be more—patient," I said humbly, ashamed that this marvelous woman had found me so imperfect.

Her fingers carressed my ear. "Of course, Gay. We'll both try to have patience with Sandy." She took my arm and led me to a chair. "I don't know why we're standing when we could be comfortable. We'll have some tea."

I sat there feeling awkward and she said, "Good heavens, child, none of this is your fault. You've been wonderfully good."

I looked at the place where my painting, Sandy's lovely gift to me, had hung. Nothing had been put in its place and the empty spot on the wall suddenly depressed me. "I can't stay for tea, Mrs. Carlyle," I said. "Aunt Sue is expecting me."

"Oh, of course. Another time, then." She smiled warmly and we moved toward the hall. "Let's make it soon. I don't see half enough of you, Gay." She pressed my hand. "Don't worry quite so much about our Sandy."

I hadn't meant to say it, but I heard myself blurting out, "I love him and he doesn't love me and I can't *reach* him!"

She pressed my hand again and spoke soothingly. "It's all right. It's all right." And just before she closed the door behind me, she said in a light tone but with her eyes looking directly into mine, "Actually, Gay, dear, I think you ought to marry him."

I stumbled down the hall to the elevator. Marry him.

Had she said that? And yet, somehow, it didn't seem so surprising. She thought I was good for him, could help him.

On the way home I prayed like mad for some idea of how I could help Sandy. His problem seemed to me to be more than overwork. He was sick, but what could I do?

I needed to talk it over with someone, but it would frighten Aunt Sue and Mrs. Carlyle would only go on and on about artistic temperament. I wanted to take Sandy to a doctor, but which one? Dr. Horseley was an old codger type who gave shots for everything from a sore throat to mumps and he'd be out of his element here. Dr. Harvey Button? A gynecologist wasn't what Sandy needed, of course, but I felt that I could trust Dr. Button's judgment, that he would give good advice about getting the best treatment for Sandy. Then I could talk to Mrs. Carlyle again.

I decided to call Dr. Button's office the next morning and ask for an appointment, but I never did because the next morning I was in Wyoming.

In spite of the cool, peaceful moments, I remember those three days and nights as a kind of brightly-colored, fascinating whirlwind.

Mrs. Carlyle had arranged everything, plane reservations and so on, and also Aunt Sue's approval, for Sandy and his mother and me to fly to this fabulous dude ranch. We all needed vacations, she said, and deserved them, and there we were!

It was quite different from my other trip to the Rockies when Aunt Sue and I rode on a bus for days and then shared a cold cabin at Yellowstone and walked down the road half a block to the john. And even that must have put Aunt Sue in debt for quite a while.

It was a nice trip and served its purpose at the time, but now I'm spoiled. At the ranch, I had a lovely room of my own with a private bath, a view, and three closets, each one a yard square.

There was plenty of entertainment—horseback riding, sightseeing, swimming, delicious meals, singing around the campfire, hiking, movies, parties with attractive, attentive cowboys who danced well and made me realize that there were other things in life besides Sandy's moods, if you could pay for them.

And Sandy perked up the last day, too. At first he was very quiet and stayed in his room most of the time, but then on the third morning he joined me at the swimming pool wearing wonderfully wild orange-red and white striped trunks. He swam and dived beautifully, something I hadn't known about him.

He rode well, too, and looked so handsome in his jodphurs I could hardly take my eyes off him. But that night I saw him for the first time in formal clothes and I almost died, he was so magnificent.

He told me that I looked lovely in my new dress and Mrs. Carlyle said that she hoped I would keep all the clothes I'd found hanging in one of my three closets. I did keep the dress I wore that last night but decided to leave the other things, because where else would I wear sequined vests and so on, even though it was great fun wearing them there.

During that last dance, Sandy leaned down and whispered in my ear, "We've had some nifty times, haven't we, Gay?"

I felt my heart jump in my chest and when it finally settled down, it hurt. It was the way he said it that touched and excited me—wistfully, but without trying to be, as if he really meant it and nothing put on. As if he was talking to himself as much as to me, but knowing very well that I was there. He said nifty, not wonderful or great or any of the other words that might not have quite convinced me. I'd never heard him say nifty before—he didn't use slangy, old-fashioned words like that—but somehow it was exactly right and it made my heart hurt like crazy.

Flying back home, I thought of what a successful, purging trip it had been. I felt a million years younger, just barely seventeen again and Sandy, dozing with his head leaning back against the seat, seemed rested and at peace.

Mrs. Carlyle insisted that she and Sandy ride home with me even though the taxi could easily have dropped them off on the way. "Just make sure your aunt is home, dear," she said and then laughed at herself. "I know I'm being a mother hen."

Sandy and I walked around the Jag parked at the curb. I hadn't driven it for days and it looked a little lonely in the moonlight.

Aunt Sue was asleep and I went back to the porch to wave to Mrs. Carlyle. Sandy was waiting at the bottom of the steps and he smiled at me before he walked to the cab and again before he opened its door. I stood there on the porch waving and feeling quite pampered and special and very, very happy.

11

Sandy seemed in such good spirits the next day—I remember thinking that the short vacation had done us both a world of good—and I forgot about the strange days and thought only of our good memories.

There was the time, for instance, when he woke me up by throwing little pebbles against my window. No one had ever done that before and I was really intrigued. I saw him standing apart from the house, under a street light so that I could see him and not be afraid, and I dressed faster than I ever had in my life and ran out to meet him.

"I couldn't sleep," he said, "so I decided to walk. I sleep so badly—I thought if you wakened right away—you know? But if you hadn't, I'd've gone away."

To think that I could have slept on and missed him! I was delighted that he'd wanted to be with me, had seemed to need me. I was sorry that he couldn't sleep, but there was good in everything and his insomnia had brought him to me hours early.

Thank God he felt better now. He looked so handsome lying there on the blanket with the sun shining on him and his dark eyes dreaming. His tan had deepened since the beginnings of summer and his teeth were whiter than ever in contrast.

I wanted to kiss him so badly I couldn't speak and I loved him so much I could have died. When would he love me? Would he ever?

We were alone in the woods, there was no one to bother us. I thought, what shall I do.

I picked up his guitar and strummed it, very softly, and watched his face. His expression didn't change so I began to sing, still very softly. "Black is the color of my true love's hair, His lips are wondrous rosy fair—I love my love and well he knows, I love the ground whereon he goes—but still I hope the time will come when you and I shall be as one."

Sandy was smiling just a little and I couldn't help it—I put down the guitar and went to lie beside him. I loved him more than anything in the world and I kissed his mouth and it was so wonderful, soft and exciting.

I closed my eyes and touched him and prayed that he would kiss me and love me. I waited and then opened my eyes when I felt him move away.

He was sitting up and looking down at me. His eyes were very black and hard and cold. Then his mouth twisted and he said, "You?"

It was the most contemptuous sound I'd ever heard in my life and it made me feel numb. I stared at him and watched him as he stood and walked away from me, his hands playing with the fly of his trousers and opening it and he stood there by the car with the fly open and his hands so busy, absorbed in what he was doing. I knew he didn't want me or anyone, only himself. Or maybe he hadn't forgotten me but was talking to me, telling me this way deliberately, I didn't know, but I couldn't stay there.

I stumbled to my feet and over the blanket and ran through the woods, between the trees and bumped into one of them. I ran and ran.

I barely remember getting out of the woods and hitchhiking home. The man who gave me the ride was as silent as I was. He asked me where I wanted to get off and I told him and these were the only words either of us spoke. I was really grateful to him for minding his own business as I couldn't have talked about what had happened and I wasn't in any shape to make up a story.

I huddled in my room for quite a while, like a wounded animal, I guess. I kept moaning, but not aloud, only inside, until finally I realized that I'd better go back and drive Sandy home. He wasn't able, in some ways, to take care of himself, couldn't see well enough to drive.

I knew I'd have to borrow Fritz's car, take Sandy home and return the Dodge, and then hitchhike back for the Jaguar.

Fritz's door was closed but I could hear him moving around inside his room. I knocked and waited, trying to look pleasant because I really needed to use the Dodge.

He blinked when he saw me and then his eyes got this crafty look and his voice became pretty arrogant. "Well, well, there's Goldilocks. What's the matter, honey—your classy Jag break down?"

"That's about it, Fritz." I tried to sound friendly. "How about letting me use your car for just a little while? I'll bring it back in an hour, I promise."

"I knew that had to be it." His lip curled like a dog's. "I'm good enough to talk to when you want something, right?"

"Look, Fritz, just one measly hour."

He took the car keys out of his pocket and dangled them in front of my face but of course he held on to them. "What's it worth to you, babe?"

I was in a hurry now—Sandy might try to drive himself home—and I couldn't count on a quick hitchhiked ride back to the woods. "I'll give you five dollars." I didn't have five dollars, so I added, "When I get back."

"You'll give me more than that, cookie," he said and leaned toward me. "And right now."

I snatched the keys out of his hand and ran down the hall, but he caught up with me before I could get the front door open. He gripped my wrist with one hand and pulled my hair with the other, bending me way back, and it all surprised and hurt so much that I yelled.

"Shut up!" His face was almost touching mine—his little gray eyes were all I could see—and his breath made me want to throw up. "Damn you, shut your trap!"

I opened my mouth to yell again when there was a thudding sound behind us. Fritz's little eyes rolled up and over and wavered for a moment and then he let me go so abruptly that I almost fell.

When I straightened and turned around there was Aunt Sue standing in the middle of the stairs looking like a politician on TV before the volume is turned up, with her mouth opening and closing and no sound coming out. A big can of cleanser was still rolling a little beside the bottom step.

"Why you—" Aunt Sue gasped twice before she could go on. She gasped and glared at Fritz. "You—you *light-eyed bastard!*"

It was my turn to gasp. I'd never in my life heard Aunt Sue use a word like bastard. I could hear a door opening on the second floor. Fritz picked up the can of cleanser and, blinking foolishly, held it up to her as she came down the stairs. Aunt Sue stopped on the last step and knocked the can out of his hand.

"You pack up and get out of here!" Her voice was higher and louder than usual, but she wasn't screaming, not quite. "Right now, you hear? If you're not out of here in twenty minutes, I'll call the police!"

"Now—now—" Fritz held up his hands as if to protect himself and, without taking his eyes off Aunt Sue, nodded toward me. "It's *her* fault. She—"

I didn't wait to hear any more but dashed outside with the keys and leaped into the Dodge. The motor stalled twice but I finally got it going and drove off just as Fritz shot out the door (with Aunt Sue right behind him) and shook his fist at me, really shook his fist, like the villain in a melodrama, and shouted something I couldn't hear.

Sandy was gone when I got there, and so was the Jaguar. He had taken the blanket, hamper, and guitar, and only the hammock marked our special place in the glen. It was the only trace of him and the woods seemed terribly lonely.

I hoped he would not have an accident driving home.

I started to leave and then suddenly thought of something. I walked over to the hammock and there in the center of it, weighted down with his jackknife and his two palette knives, were several sheets of paper torn from Sandy's sketching pad.

My breath shook as I exhaled. I sat down on the ground to read my mail. There was a charcoal sketch of a devil at the top of the first page and the rest of the pages were covered with large, scrawled letters. In red ink he had written:

"Dear Gay,

I think the best thing for you to do is to carry a combination of cream cheese and bleu cheese in a medium-sized ball in a section of your purse.

Then we shall never be thirsty, although a spoon would help.

But never a straw. Never on Wednesday.

Of course it is all truly blue.

I mean it. You can be perfectly sure of that.

Don't melt your wax, Icarus.

Where's your head, boy?

Gone — bashed in.

Where did all the miniheads go?

To the cave mines, every one.

Lick salt? Who has seen the tale?

The wee Canuck. Petit Jacques. Head stove in. Who dun it? I, said the little green weevil on your shoulder. Mit meinen hatchet. Merci. Mercy.

My toe is a catgut. Who says you are worse?

Yours very truly,
Alexander Sanford Carlyle III
(Sandy to you)

N.B. (Who is Gay?)
Ad hunkus glorium
 # (The End)"

I thought, Oh God, Sandy, and drove the old Dodge out of the woods and back home.

Fritz was standing at the curb with his suitcases beside him. "Listen, you little bitch!" he yelled at me. "You car thief! I'm gonna call the cops!"

He actually shook his fist again. What a ridiculous person!

I got out of the car and threw the keys toward him. "You do that," I said. "You call the cops so I can tell them how you feel about seventeen-year-old girls."

He shut his mouth and he looked pale. I wasn't being strictly fair, but who cared? I watched him drive off and then I went inside, feeling hard and unsympathetic.

Aunt Sue wanted to talk, but I didn't and asked her to excuse me. When I heard her leave the kitchen I came out of my room and dialed Sandy's number.

After about six rings, Cook answered and told me that Sandy was there but that he and Mrs. Carlyle were in his studio and didn't want to be disturbed.

He was safe then. "All right, Cook. Thank you."

"Did you two have a tiff—a lover's quarrel, like?"

A lover's quarrel!

"No, Cook." And what business was it of hers, anyway? "Nothing like that."

She was silent, waiting for details, so I thanked her again and said goodbye.

I don't know how long I sat there staring at that black phone and not really seeing it. In my dreams of Sandy he had loved me and wanted me, and I guess I had confused dreams with reality.

12

Finally I called Harold. Ope was the only person I really could have talked to, but she was gone. Aunt Sue would worry and Velma might be flip and superior.

I felt that I'd lost something I'd never even had. I knew I shouldn't have been so humiliated—hadn't I known from the beginning that Sandy was beyond me? But I wished that Ope were there to tell me that I wasn't all wrong, that I'd had a right to love him.

Somehow Harold seemed to have changed since I had last seen him. Maybe it was because he simply opened the car door for me instead of falling all over himself or the fact that he'd gained some weight or that his car (which he had bought at last) was a plain dark blue instead of the yellow stripes he'd once mentioned and that, even though I knew he must be ready to burst with pride over his first car, he spoke of it quietly. "Nothing fancy and five years old, but it's in good shape."

And he said I'd changed. "You're different, Gay. More mature, I guess." He grinned. "Working at it, anyway. Your hair's great. Kind of classy, you know?"

He pulled up to the curb beside the Hanging Eye. "This is where you wanted to go, right?"

I opened the door on my side. "Right." I wanted lights and sound and company.

The first couple we saw was two boys with paint-daubed faces and the next was Velma, tricked out in a musical miniskirt and with her hair cut so that she could see, and Ray the Hood.

They motioned us over to their table. "Vel," I asked when Harold had gone to another room for our drinks and Ray was at the juke box, "what do you *see* in him?"

"Not much." She frowned at my tactlessness. "But then I don't see him much." She smiled at her play on words. "He's just a little different, that's all."

"I won't argue with you there."

"Um. Where's Prince Charming?"

"I'd rather not talk about —"

She cut in sharply. "You're the one who started the inquisition tonight, Gay."

"Okay. I'm *sorry*."

"You're sure in a funny mood."

"I *said* I was sorry." I knew I didn't really mean it, but the thought crossed my mind that I'd like to pay Sandy back for hurting me the way he had.

"So you did and yea verily, I forgive you." Velma glanced over at Ray. "He can get the pill. That ought to buck you up."

"No, thanks."

"Honest. He says he's got connections, but I suppose he breaks into drugstores."

"Forget it." And once Sandy had made me think of a faun!

"Well, what the hell." Velma was annoyed. "After all that fuss."

"It just happens to be the right time of the month, you know? I don't have a thing to worry about for the rest of this week."

"Listen, what's eating you? Why the spectacular bitterness?"

"Never mind, Vel. I really am sorry."

Harold came back with four big drinks on a little tray. "Ward eights, okay?"

"Dance with me?" Velma asked and added when he hesitated, "Please? Gay won't mind."

Harold looked at me and I shrugged. Velma got up and took his arm. Ray left the juke box and stood by the table, waiting, but I didn't look up at him and finally he sat down beside me. "What's the matter, baby, don't you think we could make it together?"

I shrugged and watched Velma exert herself on the floor.

"I think we could make it big." After a moment he said, "You thought it over? You ready to blow your mind? I'd be with you the whole way."

"Thanks for nothing."

"Scared? Look, a crack-up you won't get. Not with me."

"What's so special about you?" Why was I even talking to him? I sat there and listened until Harold and Velma came back, but since I hadn't taken my cues, Ray was pouting. I took a long swallow of my drink.

"I was just telling Harold about my devastating experience at the beauty shoppy." Velma was flushed from the dance. "Moth-ah insisted on coming with me, of course." She imitated her mother's worried frown and high-pitched voice. "'Those girls have no taste.' What she wanted was to make sure I got my bangs cut." She scowled. "I know she called Estelle before we left home but, naturally, she didn't let me catch her." She moved the stirrer around in her glass, brooding. "Anyway, to make a long story short, Estelle promised me she'd only cut one-eighth of an inch and I closed my eyes so hair wouldn't get in them and that absolute *bitch* cut off an *inch and a half*!"

Velma lifted her glass and set it down without drinking. "Well, I just sat there and I *cried*." She closed her mouth with a little snapping sound and glared at each of us in turn.

No one said a word. I felt sorry for her, knowing how attached she'd been to those long, shaggy bangs and seeing that she was still pretty suicidal about losing them as ordinarily she would know better than to tell a story like that in front of males. It never fails to embarrass them if you get emotional about things you're supposed to pretend you never pay much attention to.

The silence was beginning to stretch out, so I said, "How's your job coming, Velma?"

"Same old blah." She tasted her drink and turned to Harold. "What did you say these things were? They're kind of loaded."

"Rye, I think," Harold answered. "The name got to me—Ward eight."

"Oh, great." Velma wrinkled her nose at him. "Don't you ever take a vacation from that creepy place?"

Harold shrugged. "You mean Twin Elms Villa? A permanent one next week. Then's when I start my mech course." He gulped down some of his drink and added, "Funny, but I'm going to miss some of the patients. I mean, they sort of get to you."

"Not if you're smart," Ray the Hood said.

Harold gave him a long, cool look and then shrugged again. "So I'm not so smart."

"Get to you?" Velma asked. "You mean you feel sorry for them?"

"Some of them. The schizos got it the worst, I guess. They're all hung up on voices and hallucinations and well, like, they see people's faces falling apart and beds climbing up the walls—things like that."

Ray grinned. "Sounds like a real groovy trip."

The whole evening was making me nervous and more depressed. I drank all of my Ward eight and hardly tasted the liquor, just the nice cold wetness on my tongue and down my throat.

Then I began to feel better, rather elated, with Harold's and Velma's words more or less floating on air in my ears, and I wondered why I hadn't ever tried this before. What I had been missing!

I put the empty glass on the tray and raised my eyebrows at Harold. He hesitated and looked at me hard, but I must have passed inspection because he emptied his own glass and took the tray to the bar.

Velma asked, "Ray, you want to dance?" He got up, looking surly, and moved off with her.

Harold came back with only two drinks this time, and I didn't blame him. Let Ray buy his own share and anyway, he and Velma had barely touched theirs. I reached for mine and Harold said, "Take it easy, Gay."

"I'm dehydrating."

"Well, drink some water, then. You're not in training for A.A."

"Oh, fun-nee," I said, unable to think of anything clever or even sensible. God, I was depressed, to the point where I didn't care any more what anyone thought. All I was interested in was feeling better, but I had almost finished the second Ward eight by the time I realized that it wasn't the answer.

I'd never had two drinks before. I'd never even had one real drink, only a little of Aunt Sue's wine, and I felt pretty bombed.

I sat there fairly numbly and tried to pick up on the conversation. Harold was saying, "....and then after that I'll take this diesel course and ...."

Oh God, I thought dizzily, I'll never pull out of this one. I must have made some kind of a sound about then because Harold stopped in the middle of a sentence and asked, "Gay, are you all right?"

I managed to say what I was thinking, that I needed some air. I guess I said it well enough since none of the others seemed to think anything was wrong. It's strange, isn't it, Sandy, I remember thinking, how you can be in a world of your own and still make the rest of them think you're in theirs?

When Harold and I said goodnight and walked out of the Eye nothing seemed quite real to me, except possibly the evil look Ray shot at me and his gesture with his cigarette. I knew he would like to burn me with it for leaving with Harold instead of with him.

Harold drove out into the country a way and maybe in the back of my mind I knew what was going to happen because I kept thinking of a nightmare I've had two or three times. The moon was fairly bright and I could see Harold's profile quite clearly, but in the nightmare I am always alone and walking down a pitch black street, in a residential part of some unknown city. I am completely lost, and frightened. Then, to add to my terror, I become aware that someone evil is following me and is almost upon me. I look around frantically for help or a place to run or hide but I can just barely see outlines of houses in the night and there are no lights anywhere. I run up on a dark porch but the pursuer is right behind me.

Then I wake up, panicked, and I hurry, still half asleep, to make the dream come out all right, to escape somehow.

I shuddered, thinking of it. "Somebody walk over your grave?" Harold asked.

"I guess," I answered, and he began to whistle.

He parked and asked how I felt. I shrugged, but actually I was still a little dizzy. Harold put his arm around me and I tensed up. Then I remember thinking, what's the use? or something like that, and letting my body relax. As soon as I did this, Harold kissed me and kept on kissing me and I kept thinking, what's the difference?

Harold's eyes were so bright they seemed to stab into me and his forehead against my cheek felt hot, as if his brain was burning up.

I don't remember everything—his hands moving over me, I said "ouch" once and he said, "Gee, I'm sorry, Gay," and how I wished afterward that I could turn time back and relive it differently.

And all the way home I felt worse than ever, really down, and neither of us said anything. My thoughts went round and round. Well, I never expected it to be the way it's described in books—I'm sure it's okay, but I'll still have to count the days to the next period—Why did it have to be Harold?—Why this?—Why didn't I cry for hours or slam doors or scream or get a lot drunker or shoot myself or drop acid?—Why this instead?—Because I'd known him for so long and he was there at the right time?—Because I knew how he felt about me and in some crazy way I thought I owed him something?—Sandy, why did you have to send me away?

My room was filled with yellow roses, so many they seemed to be exploding all over the room. An ocean of flowers like that should have cheered me up, I suppose, especially since the card said they were from Sandy. The trouble was, I was sure that he'd had nothing to do with sending the roses and that Mrs. Carlyle was once again trying to spare my feelings.

After a while Harold called. "Uh, Gay. Listen, I've been thinking—I mean, you know, do you want us to get married or anything?"

"Oh, Harold."

"Things would be tight for a while, but after a couple of years I'd be earning a lot more."

"I appreciate your offer, Harold." We were being quite formal about it all. "But I couldn't. I mean, it wouldn't work out. Thank you anyway." Why should I marry Harold? I'd never wanted him. All I could think of was Sandy.

"Are you sure?"

"Yes." He'd really wanted me with rose bushes on the back fence and an apron tied under my chin, but that wasn't what he'd got.

"Well, okay. If you're sure."

"I'm sure. Look, Harold, do you mind if I sign off? It's been a long night."

He was silent and I said, "Oh. I mean —"

"Yeh, I know. Sure. Well, goodnight, Gay. See you."

"Goodbye, Harold."

I asked myself what had happened, but there didn't seem to be much of an answer. It was easy to put down hoods like Ray, but somebody like good old Harold could sort of sneak up on you.

Well, forget it. Try to forget it.

I couldn't sleep so I read, going over and over the same lines without taking in the sense of them. I wanted to see Sandy. He didn't care about me, but that didn't mean I'd stopped loving him. I thought about calling him or going to his apartment. I could think of some excuse. I thought, I can't do that. I guess not. Of course not. I've got a little pride, I hope, and anyway, it wouldn't work. I can't make him see me or talk to me, can't make him love me. I can't. Can I?

I kept turning the pages of the book, and smelling those roses, and finally, about the time the sun was beginning to rise, I fell asleep and dreamed of a painting, a gray desert, with one big blob of red blood in the middle of it, the loneliest, most barren, most depressing and frightening thing I had ever seen.

Then I dreamed that Sandy and I were in the woods and he said, "You have too many fantasies, Gay, dear. Nothing could be that fine."

Then he said, "Well, answer the phone."

I thought he was joking, but when I chuckled he glared at me. "Answer it, answer it."

"But good heavens, Sandy, here in the woods—a *telephone?*"

We stared at each other. At last he frowned and dropped his eyes. As he turned away, I heard him mutter, "Let the goddamned thing ring then. What do I care?"

13

The phone kept ringing and ringing and finally I realized that I was not dreaming the sound. I struggled out of bed and into the kitchen to answer it. Aunt Sue came in from her room just as I lifted the receiver and croaked out a hello.

"Gay? I'm sorry to call you so early," Mrs. Carlyle said, "but I do want to see you and I felt that I could count on you."

"Oh." Somehow I hadn't expected to hear from her, and she sounded upset. "Of course, Mrs. Carlyle."

"Sandy has been taken to the hospital."

I held my breath and waited.

"He—he barricaded himself in his room and I had to —"

The conversation seemed to have become disconnected. I gripped the phone to keep it from moving in my hand.

"I had to," she repeated.

"What's wrong?" Aunt Sue asked.

I held my hand over the mouthpiece. "Sandy's in the hospital."

"Oh, my, what —?" Her face got pale. "A car accident?"

"No, Aunt Sue, he's sick." It was the first time I'd said it aloud. "Sandy is sick."

"You understand, don't you, Gay?" Mrs. Carlyle asked. "I had to put him there."

I took my hand from the mouthpiece. "He's at Twin Elms Villa, isn't he, Mrs. Carlyle?"

"Twin Elms!" Aunt Sue stared at me. "Why, that's for — for —"

I nodded to her. It's hard to say "crazy people." It's even hard to say "mental patients" when you are talking about someone you know.

"Mrs. Carlyle," I said, "I'll be right there. I'll be with you in a few minutes, as soon as I can."

"Of course you must go," Aunt Sue said but I was already back in my room, hastily throwing on clothes.

Any other time there would have been at least one taxi cruising near our corner but this morning none was in sight and after running two blocks I stopped and waited for a bus.

We were half way downtown before I saw a cab. I pulled the cord and leaped off the bus and hailed the cab and finally arrived at Sandy's.

Cook answered the door and began speaking in a rush. "I knew he was heading for real trouble when the detectives brought him back last week. The poor boy was scared to death and he didn't hardly know where he was."

"Cook, please." I started past her through the hall. "I have to see Mrs. Carlyle."

"She's in his room."

The room was a wreck — chairs and tables upended and broken, vases shattered, torn draperies, the wallpaper ripped. I remembered the knives Sandy had left in the hammock yesterday. Had he known this was going to happen?

Mrs. Carlyle was sitting on the bed, staring at the door. "He wouldn't let me in," she said. "He pushed this —" She touched the edge of the mattress with her forefinger —" up against the door, and I could hear him throwing things, books, bowls —"

I sat down beside her and put my hand on her shoulder, knowing that if she hadn't looked so bleak I would have been crying. In giving her support I kept myself from breaking down.

"And shouting, calling me names—obscenities—"

"Why?" I asked. "Mrs. Carlyle, why?"

But she only shook her head.

"Hadn't you expected—well, not this —" I glanced up at a hole in the wall and the plaster cracked around it— "but didn't you see that he—that he had problems?"

"Oh, yes," she said softly, almost as if she was talking to herself. "He was like this before, but I thought—I hoped this time he wouldn't—give in."

Before. This time. Oh God.

"He was nineteen," she said and looked down at her hands on the mattress.

"Was? Sandy?" I couldn't take it in. "You mean before—the other time?"

She nodded.

"But he's—I mean, I thought he was nineteen *now*."

"He's twenty-six."

"*Twenty-six!*"

"Yes—yes."

"But he looks—he looks so young."

"Yes—it's as if part of him remained at that age."

I looked down at my own hands. At nineteen, I thought, he had had more promise. Finally, I said, "Mrs. Carlyle, if you knew he was—was becoming ill—I mean, I was alone with him so much, painting in the woods. You knew that."

She raised her eyes and looked at me steadily. "My dear Gay, Sandy has never in his life hurt a soul."

Hasn't he? I thought, but I couldn't explain that I felt damaged, couldn't blame my own behavior on Sandy.

She looked at me for another moment and then said, "He's tried so hard. I could see him trying."

"But what—what is it? Why does Sandy, why did he—what's *wrong* with him?"

"He's been diagnosed as a schizophrenic."

"Schi —"

I watched her draw away from me, shrink away, and I lowered my eyes to hide what was making her cringe.

After a while she said, "I'm sorry, Gay. I thought you knew."

I sat there feeling weak and more alone than I had ever felt in my life. The room seemed edged in black and unreal. "How would I know?"

"Of course. Of course you wouldn't. I forgot that you weren't a part of our family." She raised her hand and dropped it. "I'm afraid I've been thinking of you as one of us all along."

Now I wanted to pull away from her. What if I spoke about artistic temperament? But maybe that wasn't fair. I didn't know.

"He was in his second year at school," she said. "His grades were fairly good the first year and I thought he would finish college, but then he failed the second year. He couldn't seem to concentrate and he was so tired and depressed. He's never wanted to return and I've never pressed him." Her eyes moved, searching the room, for what, I wondered. "When he's well, he's happy with his painting and his music."

"I think you should have told me before."

"Yes—yes." Her eyes were big and dark. "I'm trying to tell you now, Gay."

I nodded and neither of us spoke for a while.

"When he—isn't well, the world seems distorted to him. For a time he refused to look into a mirror or to let anyone see him. He hid his face from me and stayed in his room. He said nothing but I felt that he thought he had grown ugly."

The times he had moved away from me; had I seemed like a monster to him?

"His perception is faulty."

Yes. He doesn't see or hear the way it really is. He can't steer a car and he tells me to shut up.

"Hallucinations."

I knew only a little about schizophrenia. I was learning more. The long silences—had Sandy been listening to voices no one else could hear and seeing things no one else could see?

"I told him—all summer I told him not to talk about what he saw and heard and felt. Other people wouldn't understand. Tell me when we are alone."

He never really trusted me. Not me, only Mother.

"Concentrate on what people are saying. Try to understand a key word. When you have the subject in mind, you can make a comment."

"Books?" Sandy had said. "I don't think books should be censored.

"Poetry? Do you like poetry? Then I'll give you this book."

I had thought they were real, our times together when I told him everything and he had listened so closely. How much sense had he made out of my chatter?

Oh Sandy, if I'd known I wouldn't have talked so much, and I'd have said every word slowly and clearly.

Mrs. Carlyle came toward me again, sensing, I suppose, that horror had changed to pity.

She'd built a padded world around him, to keep him from his cell. I wanted to beat her and lock her up for hurting both of us, Sandy and me. She seemed as sick as he was.

I almost screamed at her, "Can't you *help* him? There must be something to do!"

But she shook her head.

"Is that all?" I wanted to be away from her. I wanted to go to Sandy.

"Depression," she said. "So often. Last night he put his belt around his neck and tried to choke himself."

He was suffering and I couldn't help him. I closed my eyes.

When she spoke again I looked at her. I knew that she was choosing her words carefully, gauging how far she could go, how much I could take.

Had he ever said to her, "What if I say something foolish or strange?" And did she answer, "Don't worry so much, Sandy. Just do the best you can."

Had she added, "Gay loves you and will always give you the benefit of any doubt."

Apparently she decided that I'd had enough for a while, as she touched my shoulder and then turned away in silence.

I needed to be alone, I needed time to think. I wanted to say "Goodbye" and heard myself saying, "I'm sorry."

"It isn't your fault."

I hadn't said it was, but I understood that she felt I had failed him, and I felt a wave of guilt. And yet, what could I have done?

"I want to see Sandy."

"Not just yet, dear. Wait until he's better."

I shook my head and dug in my heels.

"He wouldn't recognize you now."

"Would he know you?"

She gave me a pitying look. "No." She rose when I did and added, "Do take the car and go to the hospital, though, Gay. Ask for Dr. Randolph. I'll call and tell him to expect you. I'm sure he can explain everything to you better than I have."

She paused and put her hand on my shoulder. "I've told you all this, dear, because I know you love him."

"Yes, I do," I said. "I do love Sandy."

We smiled a little at each other then, but her hand on my shoulder weighed a ton.

Her answers hadn't satisfied me and the psychiatrist would tell me only what they wanted me to know. I wanted to see Sandy, needed desperately to see for myself how he was and make certain that he was being well cared for.

I parked the Jaguar in the visitors' lot and walked toward the employees' entrance. I was determined to see Sandy, and Harold couldn't refuse to help me.

14

It seemed strange to see Harold in a white jacket and carrying a bunch of keys on a big ring. I must have startled him, showing up like that, but he tried not to show it, tried to act like a man of the world—until I told him why I had come.

"Aw, Gay." I had flagged him down in the hall, and now he glanced nervously up and down the empty length of it. "It's against the rules to take anybody down to the disturbed ward."

I waited, hating to have to ask him for this favor, because he had no choice. He couldn't refuse me, and when he'd gone through a list of objections, he would take me to Sandy.

"He's in no shape for visitors, Gay—I wouldn't kid you about that."

"Please, Harold."

"No. You don't know what you're asking."

"Harold —"

"Look, Gay. For one thing, he cut his —" He stopped and looked away.

"What?" I clutched at his sleeve and coffee spilled from the paper cup in his hand.

"His, uh, you know—penis."

Oh. Oh, God. "Harold, are you sure? I mean, did he mu—mutilate himself? There? I mean—"

"He tried to cut off his dick," Harold said flatly. "I didn't have to read that in his work-up. It's all over the hospital."

I felt cold all over. I thought wildly of going to everyone who'd ever known Sandy—the waiters, the ushers, even carnival freaks, so they could tell me that it wasn't true. Their good will, their smiles and help had been bought, yes, but surely they had some real affection for him, surely they knew that he couldn't have done this to himself.

"That's why his mother had him brought in," Harold was saying. "All that blood got to her."

I stood there numbly. Had I had anything to do with Sandy's cutting himself? Had I pushed him over the brink by throwing myself at him?

"From what I hear," Harold said, "she always keeps him out till the last minute—figures she can handle him."

"Always? I know he was here before, but —" Once before wasn't always.

"Yeah, twice. Last time was a year ago."

Three times from nineteen to twenty-six? "But that's—chronic."

Harold nodded. "And the worst part is nothing works on him—therapy, drugs—even the new stuff—nothing takes."

"Harold, I've got to see him."

"Huh uh. No."

"I *know* he's sick."

"You don't know the half of it. You should hear him howl—just like a wolf."

I winced. "Harold, listen. I've *got* to see him. If I ever meant anything to you —"

His face turned brick red and I knew that I was the one who should have been blushing, but I couldn't afford a sense of guilt just then. I had to get to Sandy.

"Harold—look, I'll get on my knees and *beg* you—"

"All right," he said roughly, without looking at me. "But remember you *asked*. You hear, Gay? You *asked* me to take you to him."

"I begged you," I said. "That's understood."

"Stay here." He walked away, turning off to the right. I heard his footsteps go down the hall and then his voice. "Hey, Dan, you take the tray in to Carlyle yet?"

"No." The new voice was surly. "Took you long enough."

"Yeah, long coffee line. Go ahead and drink it—I'll take in the tray."

"Oh, hell, man, you didn't take that long." But his voice lost some of the surliness. "It's my turn."

"No sweat." I heard a rattle of dishes and then footsteps, and Harold came around the corner and nodded to me to follow. He was walking so fast that I could hardly keep him in sight and I was afraid he would go around a corner and be lost before I could catch up.

At each turn, though, he stopped and looked up and down the hall and then motioned to me to hurry, to be quiet.

At last he stopped and spoke in a low voice. "He's down there." He pointed to a door at the end of the short hall.

I looked at the bars across the small hole in the door. Sandy, who had had so much, now had this cell with a barred window. And with all the deprivation, no privacy. Anyone walking down this hall could look in and stare at him.

"You still want to see him?" Harold asked, and I nodded. "You sure?"

"I'm sure."

"He's in bad shape, Gay."

I started to walk toward the door and Harold followed. "I'm supposed to try to feed him." He balanced the tray on his left arm and singled out a key with his right hand.

"Now, listen, Gay." He kept his voice way down. "We're supposed to work in pairs down here, but Dan and I don't usually bother. If we need help we yell and the other one comes running, see? So if it starts to get rough, you duck around the corner and keep going down the hall, okay? There's a john at the end and nobody'll see you. I'll rap shave and a haircut and steer you out later."

I nodded and Harold asked through the bars, "How about some breakfast, Mr. Carlyle?"

There was no answer, only a shuffling sound from within the cell. Harold unlocked the door and we went inside.

The hall was dark and narrow but clean. The cell was filthy and the stench made me gag.

Sandy, in a straitjacket, crouched in a corner. I tried to smile at him but he looked right through me. Bright dots of oil paint spattered his cheeks and chin and forehead. "Hex signs," Harold said, "to ward off the devils. He had them when he was admitted and he won't let us take them off."

Then I noticed the brown smears on Sandy's face and hands and on the walls and realized where the terrible smell was coming from. I stared at his mouth.

"He'd swallow nails if we'd let him," Harold said.

I retched. I tried not to but I couldn't help it. This was Sandy glaring at us, Sandy with feces on his beautiful mouth and caked under his fingernails. I looked away from him and whispered, "He doesn't even know me."

"What'd you expect?"

I snapped back at Harold. "Why isn't he kept clean? Why is he in that awful jacket?"

"We had to—he was wild. You see what he did to the walls."

"Oh, who *cares* about the walls?" I was ready to cry. I was angry and sad and all mixed up.

"He was tearing off his bandage, too," Harold said. "The cut isn't deep, but we can't let him mess it up any more."

"What did he use?" I thought again of the knives Sandy had left in the hammock. Had this been the real message?

Harold looked at me. "You'd better leave, Gay. Go on down the hall to the john and I'll catch up with you after I feed him."

I shook my head. I wanted to leave and felt guilty about wanting to leave. I gagged again and asked, "Don't you ever clean him up?"

"Yeah, but not every goddam minute," Harold answered. "After he eats, we will. Again.

"I'm sorry, Gay," he added then, awkwardly. "I know you liked him."

Liked him! For a second nothing seemed real. It was all a bad dream and I would surely wake up.

Harold dug a spoon into a mound of applesauce and approached Sandy with it. Sandy would not open his mouth and Harold coaxed, "Better eat up, Mr. Carlyle. No more till lunch."

Suddenly Sandy lunged, butting with his head and knocking the tray from Harold's hands and scattering food and dishes around the cell. "Goddam it," Harold said and wiped applesauce out of his eyes.

Sandy stood in the middle of the room shouting at us, calling us all kinds of obscene names. I backed away then, to the door, even though Sandy did not move toward me. What was he seeing to make him scream like that? What did he think was happening, who was after him to make him so mad and so scared?

"Go on, get out," Harold said. "He could hurt you."

I didn't need to be told twice, then, but I couldn't seem to move, couldn't take my eyes off Sandy. Harold gave me a push in the right direction, but it only made me stumble and I crashed into a big, rough-looking young man coming into the cell.

"What's going on?" he asked, "and who the hell is *she*?"

"She's with me, Dan." Harold motioned for me to go out. "Just leaving."

"Yeah?" Dan looked at me as if I belonged in a cell, too, and then he turned back to Harold and waved his thumb at Sandy who had stopped screaming and was standing ridigly, glaring at Dan. "He giving you trouble?"

"Tried to," Harold said, and I went out of the cell, moving fast now, and down the hall, but not to the john. I backtracked, lost my way once, and finally ran past the attendants' station, around a corner, and out the employees' entrance. I felt that I couldn't stand to be in the building a minute longer. I had to have fresh air and sun and a feeling of balance.

15

I sat in the car and tried to think.

Sandy in the filthy cell. I retched, remembering, and got out of the car to breathe deeply.

The black dream that was his life. Black is the color. This was the end of the song:

> "I go now to Clyde to mourn and weep
> But satisfied I never could sleep.
> I'll write to you in a few short lines
> I'll suffer death ten thousand times."

It must be hell not to be sure of what you are seeing or hearing or thinking or feeling, hell to be so afraid.

Maybe, I thought, when he cut himself, he wasn't trying to get rid of something but trying to get hold, to *feel* something. I could understand this but the Sandy who screamed and smeared feces was so different from the one I'd known and loved.

It was like death in that cell.

No one was to blame—not Mrs. Carlyle or Sandy or myself. We all did what we had to do, and I might have gone along with the plan if I hadn't seen this different Sandy.

The summer seemed to whirl around me—at the very beginning of it Sandy had said, "You could get married, Gay."

Poor, poor Sandy. He could never forget that he needed a keeper.

I'd been only an apprentice but someday Sandy and everything he owned could be mine. I'd never miss him again, not even for a day.

I remembered Sandy's old girlfriend Carla and her pitying look that night in the restaurant. How many others had there been? How many had not measured up or had decided that belonging wasn't worth the dues?

Mrs. Carlyle must have gone through all the Carlas she could find—girls Sandy had gone to school with, girls she recognized—before she decided to settle for me. Me—caring, healthy, dependable, dazzled. . .

Someone who didn't seem to feel a need to grow. . .

I was young and could take care of Sandy forever. I wouldn't die first, as she would.

I would probably never be offered a better-paying job. Or one with better fringe benefits. Or with more security.

Everything but freedom, pride, love.

What had made me think everything was going to be handed to me, anyway? I'd have to get out and make my own life. And I wanted to.

I felt a little dizzy, a little sick, thinking of what I'd almost missed.

I'd loved Sandy but now I asked what is love and knew that I wasn't near the answer.

I'd loved him and I couldn't turn this off like a water tap, but could I give up being loved? He would never love me, would never be able to.

Sandy lived in a world that didn't exist, a world full of strange colors and smells and feelings, and no room in it for me.

I couldn't take it. I decided to go on down to the university and register. If I was too late I'd get a job there in town and wait for the second semester. It would be a new life, a new challenge, and maybe, this next time, I'd be able to make it.

I drove to the Carlyle apartment and parked the Jag in front of the building. Mrs. Carlyle wasn't in, so I left the car keys with Cook who kept me standing in the hall while she chattered on and on until finally I broke in and said, "The worst part is that he's so unhappy and there isn't a thing he or I or anyone else can do about it."

"He's all alone with it in the long run, that's for sure."

She went on talking and I stood there thinking about the little rose garden next to Sandy's studio, about how I would like to go look at the tiny, pampered roses and the wide view of the city and then jump off the edge of the terrace and land face down on the sidewalk and never have to think or feel again.

Cook stopped talking long enough to take a breath and I asked her to say goodbye to Mrs. Carlyle for me as I would be going away.

Then I went back to Aunt Sue's to pack.